Wakefield Press

Black Dust Dancing

Tracy Crisp is a writer and stand-up comedian. Her written work has been published in *Best Australian Stories 2007*, *Griffith REVIEW* and *Island*. She started writing and performing comedy in the lead-up to her midlife crisis, and was a national finalist in the Raw Comedy Competition 2007. She currently divides her time between Adelaide, Abu Dhabi and Kangaroo Island. She has two young boys.

T0359206

Black Dust Dancing

TRACY CRISP

Wakefield
Press

Wakefield Press
1 The Parade West
Kent Town
South Australia 5067
www.wakefieldpress.com.au

First published 2009

Designed by Liz Nicholson, designBITE
Typeset by Clinton Ellicott, Wakefield Press
Printed in Australia by Griffin Press, Adelaide

National Library of Australia Cataloguing-in-Publication entry

Author: Crisp, Tracy.
Title: Black dust dancing/Tracy Crisp.
ISBN: 978 1 86254 827 5.
Dewey Number: A823.4

Government
of South Australia

Arts SA

fox creek
wines

Publication of this book was assisted by the
Commonwealth Government through the
Australia Council, its arts funding and advisory body.

For my mum, Vivienne

'Stick to your guns, kids'

ACKNOWLEDGEMENTS

Thank you to Arts SA for a grant provided at the beginning of this project; to Varuna, especially for a place in the LongLines programme; and to Clare, Michael and Kathy for your generous editorial guidance and advice. Thank you to Adrian. For everything.

And thank you to my dad, Denis. He didn't get to read it, but he was with me every step of the way.

CHAPTER ONE

'God, Mum, do you have to smoke while you're driving?'

'Shut up, Sophie,' Caro said. Her heart was thumping, but it was okay, the car had swerved, that was all. Some of the tyres had touched the gravel, but the car hadn't left the road. She took a drag on the cigarette. May as well smoke it now it was lit.

'It felt worse than it was,' she said, 'because we've got the trailer on the back.' She glanced at Sophie, and she smiled, but Sophie turned away and stared through the window on the side. Caro sighed. A person so angry shouldn't wear that much black.

She shouldn't have spoken to Sophie like that. She took another drag. It was the heat that did it, and she was so tired. And Christmas had lingered, of course. Christmas had made them both feel worse.

She tapped her hands on the steering wheel, clicked her tongue to the music, the crunch of the car on the gravel still in her ears. The radio started to crackle. Caro leaned in, tried to tune it to something else, then turned it off.

'Thank God for that,' Sophie said. 'I'm already sick of it. God knows what I'm supposed to listen to for a year.'

That's all Sophie said when Caro told her about the move. They don't even get FM up there, Sophie had told her. There's only two channels on TV, and one of them's the ABC. Sophie's lip had curled, of course, but Caro had decided that no amount of that would make her change her mind. It's only for a year. We'll come back for you to do year twelve. The change will do us good.

Caro pulled in at a Port Wakefield roadhouse. They would fill up with petrol, then go inside for lunch, cool down, clear the wind from their ears, rest their eyes from the sun. Caro had already decided to let Sophie buy whatever she wanted, no matter what it cost or might do to her teeth.

She drove away from the petrol pump and parked down the side so she wouldn't have to reverse when they left. She had hardly ever towed the trailer before and jackknife was a pretty descriptive word. There was hardly anyone around. No need to wind the windows up or lock the door. The hot wind knotted her hair. Sophie walked two steps behind as they entered the roadhouse cafe, its doors held open with bricks, a loud fan moving the hot air around.

A family sat at a table in the corner. Two boys, ten and twelve, Caro guessed. The woman caught Caro's eye in a hot-day glance.

'Air-conditioner's stuffed,' announced the woman behind the counter, her face glowing with sweat. She did not get off her stool.

Sophie asked for chips and a hot dog with sauce.

'It's a bit hot for chips, isn't it?'

'You said I can have whatever I want.'

Stay quiet, Caro thought as she picked a curried egg sandwich off the tray. Thin white bread, stuffed so full that egg oozed against the plastic wrap.

To escape the stink of yesterday's chip fat, she led Sophie to a concrete bench outside where they squeezed themselves into the small shady patch, Caro on one side, Sophie the other.

They did not speak.

The egg in the sandwich was gritty with curry that had not been properly stirred and the bread dried in the wind as she nibbled. A stench rose from a bin a few steps away and seagulls began to flock. Sophie threw them some chips and more arrived, dipping their necks to squawk and scare each other away.

'Don't do that. Seagulls are horrible birds.'

Sophie threw another chip.

'Did you hear what I said?'

It was too late, the birds would not leave now. They pecked at each other, sat on the end of the table, flew overhead.

'We're going.' Caro wrapped the plastic back around the sandwich, stretched it tight and threw it in the bin.

'Can I have an ice-cream?'

'No. You don't deserve one now.'

Stupid, childish words, she wished she could take them back. When Sean was around, she had never spoken like that.

'What? Why?'

'Oh, come on,' she said as she let Sophie follow her back into the roadhouse. She'd change her mind, but she wouldn't apologise.

Caro's own ice-cream was melting by the time she was back in the car. She opened the door and sat on the front seat with her legs outside, stretched wide apart.

'Hello.' It was the woman from inside the cafe, the other mother. 'Where you going?' the woman asked.

'Port Joseph.' Caro had said the words a thousand times before, but they sounded different today.

The woman looked at the camper trailer. 'On holidays?' she asked.

'No. We're moving there.'

'We're moving too. To Woomera. My husband's a teacher. A headmaster. Principal they call it now. It's a promotion.'

It was too hot for small talk, Caro thought, but didn't turn away.

'They say the Sturt desert peas are beautiful when they're out. You should come and see them. Port Joseph's not that far away. They come out in August, I think. Or maybe November. I can't remember. But you could find out. They say it's definitely worth the trip.'

'They are beautiful,' Caro said. 'We went to see them once. My husband and I.'

The woman might not have heard. 'We could have gone to Mount Gambier,' she said. 'But Roy – my husband – he says this is more adventurous.'

Caro nodded.

'He told the boys there'd be rockets and soldiers. They think it's gonna be great.'

The woman wiped the sweat off her cheeks.

'We're only going for a couple of years. And I like those desert peas.'

'They are beautiful,' Caro said, fanning her skirt up and down.

'You a teacher too?' the woman asked.

'No,' said Caro, 'but my husband was.' And then, from nowhere, 'and his best friend is.'

She put the ice-cream in her mouth, small enough now to fit then pulled it out again. She didn't like having to eat this fast. 'I'm a doctor,' she said.

'Oh.'

'It's so hot,' Sophie whined. 'Can't we go?'

Caro wondered again how people saw her when her daughter was talking to her like that. What did they say after she left? That mother has no control. She should discipline that child.

'I'd better go,' Caro said.

'Yeah. Good luck.'

'You too,' Caro said and lit another cigarette, closing her door. 'I'll look you up if I come for the desert peas.' The tow bar scraped the gutter as she pulled away, and she thought of holidays with Sean. Maybe I will, maybe I'll go and see the bloody desert peas.

Caro drove, Sophie slept, Caro lit another cigarette.

Sophie was right about the smoking, of course she was.

Caro decided she would definitely give up, once they got there, once they were settled in. She would give up the fags for good.

Caro kept her eyes on the road.

Still Sophie slept.

It was nice like this, just her and the journey. It was all about her and the car and the road. When you drive, you can always believe you're alone. Even when she sat in the passenger seat and Sean drove, even then she was alone with the promise of what might be.

We could do this again, she thought. If she had towed the trailer this far, she could do it again. Once you were driving, you hardly noticed it was there. She could get them even further north. Next holidays they could go to Quorn, Wilpena Pound. The holidays after that Leigh Creek. There was Coober Pedy, Alice Springs. Sturt's desert peas. They would camp, and it would be good. Great. The two of them at night, staring into their fire or out to the stars. They would talk about the things they would never talk about at home. They would cook toast on the grill in the mornings, and at night eat tinned peaches with tinned cream, then get into their sleeping bags smelling of smoke, and sleep solid, outside-living sleeps. She would take a photo of Sophie in the red sea of desert peas, have it enlarged to hang on her wall, and look at it every day for the rest of her life.

She would think of Sean, smile, and remember that it was having children that made it all worthwhile.

At Lochiel, she stubbed her cigarette out. The salt lakes

were lightly pink today. Once, when Sophie had measles, Caro had read her a story about children who worked in salt mines. Completely unsuitable for a girl with a fever, it had given Sophie nightmares for weeks, making her wake in dripping sweats.

Caro remembered how it had been to stroke Sophie's hair while she slept. To rub her fingers on Sophie's cheek and to brush her brow with her palm. How long had it been since she and Sophie had touched? If she couldn't remember, did that mean it had been weeks or months or years?

Heat lines shimmered ahead. The paddocks were dusty brown, just a few sticks of wheat or hay or whatever it was left in the ground.

It was a strange idea, taking Sophie back to where Sean's life began, taking up a job that might not work out, living just streets away from his mother who was trying so hard, but didn't know how to treat Caro anymore. Why move north when she hated the heat and why go to a place with a creek for a beach when it was the sea that soothed her soul?

They were driving through Crystal Brook now. Crystal Brook it is not. She smiled to herself. When she was young, that's the kind of line she would have written into her diary and waited for it to weave her a poem. Poems never came now.

Down the dip and up again. You could see a long way from the top of this hill. You could see Port Joseph from here. The silos, the saltbush flats and the smelter's stack. It was seeing it from here that made you realise how tall that stack really was. It dwarfed the silos, and the silos weren't short.

Sophie was still asleep. Her mouth was open and her head tilted too far back. She would be even grumpier than usual when she woke, and Caro wondered yet again, If Sean hadn't died, would I have left?

CHAPTER TWO

On the plane, Heidi had practised all the things she was going to say. Gorgeous beaches, tropical greens, beautiful sand. Late breakfasts, so relaxed, Pimm's and lemonade. But as soon as she stepped off the plane – even before that, just watching Adelaide through the window as they came flying in – the city's shades of purple and grey had muted her thoughts and deadened her words. Into a taxi again (four taxis altogether), along the wide flat roads lined with stone or brick houses – no more timber or verandas raised off the ground – out of the taxi and four hours on the bus.

It only took three hours to get from Queensland to Adelaide, but it was four from Adelaide to home. Mum had made a joke the night before. 'Four hours to get two hundred ks, but only three to cross three states.' It wasn't a joke when you were sitting on the bus and facing the rest of the trip breathing in musty air-conditioned air, the radio too loud and not quite tuned. Four more hours. There went the suburbs: Prospect, Gepps Cross, Bolivar and out through Wild Horse Plains. It was lucky Zac was tired from the early morning start. That made things easier. Heidi let him sleep with his head on her knees. He had grown so much but still his body was small enough to fit curled in his seat. School. In one week, he'd be starting school. She sent him thoughts: Mummy loves you, Mummy loves you, I love you, little one. She rubbed the back of her finger across his cheek while she watched the landscape pass.

Three weeks ago had it looked so flat and brown? Was the sky so bleached by the sun's harsh light? She tried to close her eyes against the paddocks and saltbush and sheep, but she couldn't do it for long. And so she watched as time and kilometres passed and she tried to practise the words again.

Mum was 'nice', 'friendly', 'calm'. That's what she'd say to Dad. Then, for Renee: 'thin', 'tanned'. And for Joel: 'she wants to meet you', which wasn't entirely a lie.

Her chest grew tighter and however hard she tried she couldn't catch her breath. She moved her hand from Zac's hip, to his shoulder, his head.

They came to the foothills. Their gentle rise gave a softened shape to the land, but still her chest was tight. When the bus dipped down into Crystal Brook her stomach lurched, and lurched again when they came to the top of the hill and she could see across to the saltbush flats, the smelter's stack, the gulf.

Here was the roadhouse where her and Renee sometimes came on Friday nights when they first learnt to drive and everything else was closed. The place where her and Dad had waited for the RAA on the only holiday they'd ever had. It was the first time she'd heard Dad swear. The Wanderer's Inn with its arched facade and high wire fence. The turn-off, the sign. Six kilometres left.

She combed her fingers through Zac's curls, but she could hardly swallow, barely breathe, the words she had practised were slipping away, nearly gone, and others were taking their place. Because, really, what was Mum? She was laughing one moment, silent the next . . . she was up till two am, awake again at five . . . she was tickling Zac, reading him stories, then all of a sudden making him go to his room.

A plane, a taxi, a bus, one day to recover, a good night's sleep and now, here she was in the salon, facing Renee and grabbing for easy words. 'Mum took us to Sea World.' She looked down at Zac after she spoke. 'You loved that, didn't you, sweetheart? Sea World.'

'It's got sharks,' Zac said. 'And people ride on the dolphins' backs.'

'Really?' Renee said. 'People ride on the dolphins? That sounds amazing.' She bent down to him. 'So you wanna watch a video out the back while Mum gets her hair done?'

Zac nodded and took Renee's hand.

'There's been no one allowed to sit in your chair while you've been gone,' Renee said to him as they walked away.

Heidi waited. She knew they were all looking and listening, hoping to catch her eye, to be the one she'd smile at, whisper to. What would Mum do? she asked herself. In her mind, Heidi raised her arms, sang, I'm back . . . I couldn't stay away, then stamped her feet, one, two, then bowed. A low, graceful bow and a sweep of her hand.

But that wasn't what Mum would do.

Mum would not have come back.

Heidi crossed her arms, uncrossed them, crossed them again. She looked out the window, made sure her forehead was not furrowed, teeth not clenched.

Were they right, all the people who'd told her not to go? Still she did not know. Because being away was good. It was. But now, being away was finished. She was back.

Would it be better not to have been?

She looked down at her hands then scraped under her fingernails with the nail of her thumb. Already the apricot colour – borrowed from Mum the night before she came home – was peeling and chipped. Heidi scraped one by one, until Renee came back.

Renee stood in front of Heidi for just a moment, then reached out and took Heidi's hand, laced her fingers around Heidi's as if this were something they'd never stopped.

Like they were eight again. Or twelve. Or even sixteen, because they'd still been doing it then. Walking through the yard at lunchtime, finding themselves a space on the lawn or against the assembly wall. Even sitting in groups, which they did from time to time, it was just the two of them. Renee's hands were rough now – because of the colours and the shampoos and the perms – but she still had a gentle hold.

She sat Heidi in the chair near the window. Heidi knew that some of the others were peering at her from under their heaters and behind their foils and using their mirrors for a sideways glance. She would be too, if she were them.

The cape swished across her shoulders and the towel scraped against her neck. Renee pulled over a stool on wheels and sat with her legs apart, hands on her knees, her arms around her bump.

Heidi looked at her in the mirror. 'You grew. The baby grew. You look good.'

'Don't start up,' Renee said. 'I've had enough of that from Mum. You're as bad as each other. Telling me about how great I'll feel, how much energy I'll get. Never told me anything about going to the toilet ten times a night and getting stretch marks. All those purple lines running underneath my stomach. You didn't tell me that. And my ankles, if you can call them that. More like tree stumps at the end of my legs. I'd stop work, only it's air-conditioned here, and Tony reckons we can't afford to get air-conditioning put in at home. Not now that we're going down to one wage.'

'I liked being pregnant,' Heidi said, and it was true, she had. Especially when Zac had started to move and kick. And when there was no more school and she had been able to lie on the couch in the afternoons and have a sleep and wake up, knowing there was a baby growing inside. She'd forgotten the swollen ankles and stretch marks. Or if she hadn't forgotten them, she didn't count them anyway.

'You got a tan,' Renee said. She ran her hand down Heidi's hair, and again, more gently still.

In the mirror, Heidi was the first to drop her eyes.

'Your hair grew. But it held it's shape okay.' Renee lifted the back of Heidi's hair then let it fall. 'I think we'll keep this shape, maybe lift the back up to the shoulders, around the sides, maybe keep the length, but chop into it, lighten it up a bit.'

She pulled Heidi's hair away from her eyes, tucked it softly behind her ears.

'I want to go short,' Heidi said. 'Really short.'

'As short as before?' Renee asked.

Heidi nodded. More than she needed to.

'Clippers up the back? Razored?'

'As short as last time. Shorter even.'

Renee used her fingers as combs. She dragged her fingers down the length of Heidi's hair, and as she got to the bottom she pulled.

'Do you want a colour?' Her voice wasn't soft. 'Cos if you're going to go short, I'll do the colour last. It's a waste otherwise. Just cutting all that colour out.'

'Do you have henna?' Heidi asked.

'Your hair's too dark. Henna won't do anything. It won't take.'

'It makes Mum's hair shine,' Heidi said. 'And her hair's the same colour as mine.'

In the sun, under the lights at night, even that night on the beach in the moon, Mum's Queensland hair had glistened, healthy and strong.

It didn't match Heidi's memory of Mum, that strong, healthy hair, because what Heidi remembered was Mum sitting on the lounge, twisting her hair around her fingers then holding the twists awkwardly in front of her eyes and all the time talking of split and brittle ends.

'It's your money,' Renee said. 'But I'm pretty sure it won't take.'

Renee sat back on her stool, her hands pressing down on her stomach.

'The baby's kicking and I'm pretty tired. Go over to the sink. I'll find someone to wash your hair.'

It wasn't the same without Renee. The water reaching her scalp and the massage around the ears – neither of them were the same. Nor was the smell of the shampoo, and the conditioner didn't feel so soft. The basin was digging into her neck and the apprentice, Nadine, was pressing too hard. Water got into Heidi's ears and, when she sat up, dribbled down the back of her neck.

Would it help, Heidi wondered, if she said to Renee, 'It's not the same without you.'

'Thanks,' Renee said when Nadine brought Heidi back to the chair.

Renee stood behind Heidi again, combing her hair in long, careful strokes, her spare hand following the comb down the back of Heidi's head.

'You sure about going short?' Renee asked.

Heidi should have learnt by now. Why hadn't she learnt? How had she forgotten that whenever she asked for her hair to go short, Renee would know that something else was going on. Heidi thought of saying no, but she had trapped herself, trapped them both. Again. She had to nod, because 'no' would mean even more than 'yes'.

Renee cut. Big cuts at first, long strands dropping to the ground.

'Did I tell you I've got the eternity ring put away?' Renee asked.

'No.'

'I went for the emerald in the end. So it's an emerald with six diamond chips. Mum liked the ruby best, but there's something about green. I like green.' Long strokes of the scissors and more hair to the floor. 'Tony's gonna pick it up the day the baby's born. And that's all I'm gonna think about when I'm in the middle of all that pain. I'm gonna close my eyes and think about the ring.'

Heidi laughed, surprising herself. 'That ring is gonna be the last thing on your mind.'

'I know. But I have to think of something . . . it makes me sick just the very thought of getting this kid out. And now, Tony's mother reckons she wants to be there. Going around bleating about her only son, waited all these years.' Renee shook her head. 'Mother-in-laws are the worst.'

Mothers-in-law, Heidi thought. It's mothers, mothers-in-law. Governors-general and mothers-in-law. It was in the year ten exam. How had Renee forgotten? Even if you didn't remember it from English, they studied all those plurals in French. Lists and lists of them. Mothers-in-law.

Renee was cutting more carefully now. Smaller snips for shape. 'It's been a while since you had your hair this short,' she said, keeping her voice low. 'A long while.'

The snips of the scissors were as small as pecks and the metal was cold on the tip of Heidi's ear.

'Nothing happened,' Heidi said. 'I didn't do anything stupid while I was away.' But she was thinking of the moment that his fingers brushed at her throat in a promise and the breeze was dense with moisture, like nothing you would feel at home. The waves roared, but ended in gentle rolls. Her head on his shoulder, his hand on her naked knee. Her heart beat fast, her breaths were shallow. It wasn't real. It didn't mean a thing. It was just a summer holiday moment. Nothing more than that.

The scissor-pecks stopped. Heidi jumped when Renee's fingers touched her neck. Goose bumps. Her eyes met Renee's again.

'Joel's gonna propose tonight, isn't he?' Heidi asked, chest tight, throat dry. Propose. It was an ugly word.

Renee nodded.

Heidi had never believed those girls who said 'it was a complete surprise . . . I had no idea . . . I mean, we'd looked at rings, but still, I never thought'. Heidi never believed them, because of course they'd known. Because you should, shouldn't you? If you know him well enough to marry him, you should know when he's going to propose. She had known that Joel was planning it, because all of a sudden he stopped talking about getting married, about getting engaged, about having kids. He had stopped talking about 'when we get our own place' and 'it will all be different then'. And on Christmas Eve, she had known that the ring was in his pocket and the words had been rehearsed.

Before he had a chance to ask, she told him she'd made a decision about Mum: I'm going to tell her I'll go. I'll go and stay with her for three weeks.

And then, once she'd told him she was going, well, then she had to go.

But now she was back, and now Joel would propose and tomorrow she would show people the ring, and they would say where's the reception and have you set a date?

'He hasn't told anyone else, has he?'

The razor scratched one final time on the back of Heidi's head.

'No.'

'If he does . . . if he asks . . . will you be my matron of honour?' Heidi asked.

'Of course,' Renee said. 'If he asks you, and if you say yes, then of course I will.' She reached for the mirror on her trolley.

If you say yes.

Renee held the mirror behind Heidi's head and Heidi nodded at the sight of the clipped and razored hair while Renee moved the mirror to the left side, the right side and then closer to the back again. Heidi nodded all the while.

It's good. It's fine. That's great.

'Did you think I'd say no?' Renee asked. She dropped the mirror. 'Did you think I wouldn't do it?'

Heidi shook her head, but she could just as honestly have nodded.

'I meant it at the time,' Renee said. 'When I said I wouldn't do it. I meant it all back then.' Renee put her hand in the small of her back, pushed her shoulders back. 'You know yesterday, I was having those Braxton Hicks contractions all afternoon. In the end, they felt so strong, I got scared the baby might be coming. I mean there's only three weeks, so technically it could. I was so scared. Asking myself, am I really ready for this, what made me think I could be a mum? You know the kind of thing.

'But then last night, I had a dream about the baby. It's the first baby dream I've had. I don't really remember the details, what we did or what the baby looked like. But the baby was there and so were you. And when I woke up, I just had this overwhelming sense that everything would be okay. And you were definitely there.'

'Right,' Heidi said.

'Did you ever have that dream when you were pregnant?' Renee asked.

A dream? About the baby? That everything would be okay? If there had been a dream like that when she was pregnant, Heidi thought she would have remembered it.

'Maybe I had something like it,' Heidi said now. 'I don't know. It was a long time ago, wasn't it?'

'Yes,' Renee agreed. 'Right. Well, I'll go mix the henna.'

Heidi swallowed. 'Maybe I'll give it a miss. I mean, if you think it won't take. I'll have a think about it, maybe come back for a different colour next week.'

Renee shrugged. 'It's up to you.'

'I'll leave it,' Heidi said.

Renee brushed at Heidi's neck with talcum powder. The brush she used was soft and so were the strokes against Heidi's neck. She took away the towel, then the cape, letting the hair fall on the floor.

Heidi stood and watched as Renee pushed and pulled a

broom in front of her. One, two, three, and in just four long strokes, she had collected most of it, so that now Heidi's hair formed one large dark pile, with shafts of blonde which must have been left from whoever had gone before.

You don't know how much hair you've got until you see it on the floor like that.

'We should've sold it,' Heidi said. And then she laughed to show it was a joke. 'You can make heaps of money selling your hair.'

'Not once it's been on the floor,' Renee said. 'Not once it's full of dust.'

CHAPTER THREE

Joel had his arm around his mother's shoulders in a way that Sean had never done. It made Libby look small. Shorter and rounder than she really was. She looked more grey too. More grey than she was before.

'It's good, it's just so good to have you here,' Libby said, so Caro let Libby hold her longer than she usually would. She even kissed Libby on the soft skin of her cheek before she pulled away. The smell of Libby's skin was still Oil of Ulan.

When she had pulled away, Caro looked again at Joel. She had forgotten, or perhaps she had never noticed before, but Joel's smile was the same as Sean's and so were his deep-brown eyes. Sean's eyes had seduced her when she was falling in love with him. Joel had been so young back then. Ten or twelve perhaps. A brother she had barely noticed was alive, let alone had deep brown eyes.

Joel hugged her just as Libby had done, only Joel's arms rested more lightly on her shoulders and she could feel his arms cross at the back of her neck. He had held her just like this, several times since Sean had died. Had he ever done it before that? If he had, Caro couldn't remember. She could smell the heat of the day through his aftershave and she did not dare close her eyes, because Joel looked, and felt, and was, so much like Sean. As his arms squeezed gently, she thought of the summer nights when she and Sean were young and didn't need sleep.

She could not stop herself. She closed her eyes and breathed him in. Joel. Or was it Sean?

If she had wanted to, she could have forgotten where they were. She could have rubbed her fingers down his spine or cupped his cheek in her hand. She could have felt for his chest, searched for his soul, given him hours of hers.

She opened her eyes.

Joel kissed her cheek as she pulled away. A soft kiss that she felt on her lips.

She smoothed at her skirt.

'And this is Heidi,' Joel said. 'My fiancée.'

Caro held out her hand to the girl, then straightaway realised how stupid it was to hold out your hand to someone so young. Especially when you met them like this at a family barbecue. At an engagement celebration. But the girl took Caro's hand in her own and gave it a shake, not firm, but not completely limp.

'It's good to meet you,' Caro said. 'At last.'

The girl hadn't come to Adelaide for Sean's funeral. It's hard for her I suppose, Libby had said, with a little boy and everything. Although you'd think . . . I mean if it was me . . . she could have found a babysitter, and then she could have come. For Joel if nothing else.

Mmm, Caro had said, because it wasn't the time for saying

anything else. Not with all those people around. People they saw every day, people they hadn't seen for years, people she had forgotten they had ever known. How did they know? How did all these people know that Sean had died? Who had told them when to come and where to go? She hadn't invited them, hadn't asked for them, had wished that they would go. Sandwiches and cakes and cups of tea that she had never made, lasagnes and bolognese sauce that she had to make freezer space for. Phone calls, letters, cards. People holding her hand, kissing her cheek and rubbing her arm. So many people, so many words. And so, whenever Libby spoke, Caro just said mmm or yes.

'I've heard a lot about you, of course,' Caro said to the girl now. The girl's lashes were long, her cheeks brushed, and her lips glossed. Her hair, short and dark, suited her high cheekbones and pointed chin. The girl was beautiful, Caro thought, but her eyes looked tired.

'All good I hope.' Her soft laugh had a jagged edge.

Is this what I was like, Caro wondered, when I was young and Sean first brought me here? She remembered not wanting to say the wrong words, not wanting to let Sean down. Standing awkwardly, not sure where to put her arms. But had she looked this distant and lost?

She tried everything she could to stay away, she remembered that. I'll just get through these new rotations, night shifts, exams, she had said to Sean. We'll talk about it tomorrow, next week, next month. She remembered how, when finally there had been no choice – we're getting married, you have to meet them now – she had come. Libby had been everything that Caro had imagined, but the town had taken her by surprise with wide flat streets and houses made of stone. She and Sean had gone for a walk and Sean took her hand. The roses were in bloom and the afternoon light was soft.

They walked around the golf course. It was the highest point above sea level, Sean said. Fifteen feet. She had no idea what that meant, but when he laughed, so did she. The golf course was square and fenced by concrete posts and three rows of sagging wire. The grass and the pine trees looked dry. They walked the length of the high school side, then turned and walked past the cul-de-sacs which people were filling with red-brick homes, bark-chip gardens and kidney-shaped swimming pools.

They like you, Sean had said and she let him believe it was true. No need to tell him of his mother's quiet but ungentle remarks when the kitchen door was closed. He already knew his mother would have preferred another girl and Caro did not need to tell him again.

I didn't know that industry would smell so sickly sweet, she had said to fill in the space while they walked. That's the slag heaps, Sean had said, and she laughed at the word. Slag. He took her to see them at the other end of the town, piles of sheeny black lined up along the wharf. They went to the museum and he bought her a pot of 'lucky slag' and she said 'lucky slag for a lucky slag' and they laughed, because it didn't matter what had been, they had all moved on. Forty cents a pot. Proceeds to the Rotary Club.

Cheap luck.

They stood in the street while she threw the slag over her shoulder and made a wish, but she hadn't thought of the wind and the black dust marked her shirt. She brushed at it and it smudged and she couldn't stop brushing, until it was all brushed in.

What did you wish for? Sean had asked.

She could remember the sound of the wind in the flags and their lanyards tapping against the poles. She could remember the sobs of the girl who had dropped her packet of chips and the pigeons that pecked at them. There was one white one, speckled grey. Caro remembered the grey of the footpath, the blue of the sky, the green of her shoes. She remembered the curve of the street and the grace it gave the town. She remembered Sean showing her the hotel where the sailors used to go and the prostitutes used to work. She had oysters kilpatrick at the footy club, and Sean had chicken kiev.

She remembered the Flinders Ranges ancient and soft, ships on the wharf, verandas of iron lace. Footpaths lined with jacarandas spaced too far apart. Boys in cars, girls on scooters, kids on bikes.

But she couldn't remember: did she answer Sean? Had she even made a wish?

'You must be Sophie,' Heidi said.

'Hi,' Sophie said, but added nothing more. Perhaps Caro had been wrong to force Sophie to come. If she was going to act so surly, maybe it would have been better to leave her at home where she couldn't annoy anyone but herself.

'And this is Zac,' Libby said. 'He's Heidi's little boy.'

The little boy burrowed further into Heidi's legs.

'He's shy,' Libby said. 'As you can see.'

'He's okay,' Joel said. 'Aren't you, mate?' He rufffled the boy's curled hair. 'Just takes a while to warm up.'

'Drinks?' Libby said. 'We've got white wine, brown lime, beer and juice.'

'A wine would be lovely,' Caro said. It would make her even more tired, but it would help her through the next few hours. She'd go straight to bed when she got home. A cool change was coming, and she could sleep in tomorrow.

'Can I have wine?' Sophie asked.

'No.'

'Why not?'

'Because I said.'

Sophie gave a deep, loud sigh.

'The pergola looks good,' Caro said, although it still looked unsettled and tacked on. It would be better when the vines had grown.

Joel had built it in the months after Sean had died. Good for him to have a project, Libby had said when she was ringing Caro every night. Helps him to keep his mind off things. But Caro was already sick of the cliches by then. They made sense for a day or a week, perhaps, but they had soon started to cloy.

A fine mist sprayed from the black tubes that lined the posts and beams. The mist never quite reached the ground or even their feet. With the spray and the plants it might have felt cool if the pavers didn't give off all that heat.

Joel handed Caro a stemmed plastic cup, filled almost to the top with yellow wine, and he held his cigarette box towards her, the lid flipped down. That was something Sean had never done. She thought for a moment of shaking her head in a 'no', of looking to Libby, of daring her to ask.

Joel shook his hand and the box in a question.

With the top row gone, the cigarette she chose slid easily from the box and Joel lit his lighter with a flick. She held her cigarette to her lips, leaned into him, heard the paper burn as she took her first drag. Standing straight again, she caught Joel's eye and used her top lip to blow the smoke towards the ground.

He smiled, then lit his own, blew his smoke into the air.

Caro heard the unsaid words, and the lilt that Libby would use.

She took another drag, then sat in the greying director's chair. The canvas had sagged so much that it made her shoulders curl. There were other chairs, there was even a new one by the tank stand, the canvas taut, the wood unstained, but she was sitting now, it would take too much to move.

'So is the stack finished?' Caro asked. She used the colloquial deliberately, but she still preferred 'chimney' to 'stack'.

'Well, yes, it's finished,' Libby said. 'It's been finished for a year. Maybe more.'

'It's so tall, isn't it?' Caro said. 'And I don't know why, but I didn't think it would be so grey.'

'I suppose you don't notice it after a while,' Libby said.

'You probably don't notice the TV towers either.' Caro

laughed. 'But they take me by surprise every time. You know when you drive over the railway bridge and you look over a sea of tall steel towers – all very final frontier, isn't it?' Caro said, and laughed again. She was the only one.

'You've got ivy growing on yours,' Caro said. Silence-filling words. 'Look how high it's gone.'

The others all turned their heads and looked, then turned slowly back to look at Caro again.

'I noticed the stack,' Heidi said. 'When I was coming back. I hadn't realised how tall it is . . . you don't, not when you're living with it every day. But it's the first sight you see, isn't it, when you come over that hill at Crystal Brook. I was surprised. I didn't know it was that beautiful,' she said.

'Beautiful?' Libby said. She looked at Heidi through half-closed eyes.

'I know what she means,' Caro said. 'The way it rises out of the flat . . .' You could say majestic, but that was too grand. 'It's serene.'

'Serene,' Heidi said. 'That's exactly it.'

Libby looked from Caro to Heidi and back again.

'Heidi's been in Queensland,' Libby said. 'Over the summer. To visit her mother.'

'Oh,' Caro said. She remembered now. Something about a mother who had disappeared. Not died, just gone. 'Queensland,' she said. 'That must have been nice.'

'Yes, it was. It was nice.'

'We saw sharks being fed, and there were people riding on the dolphins' backs.' It was Zac, his voice thin and high.

'Really?' Caro said. She smiled at him, but he didn't say anything more.

'It was good to get home again though,' Heidi said. 'I got homesick.'

A silence again. No breeze. The sky was changing colour, to become more blue and less washed-out. It would be an hour or more till the sun went down. The cool change was still nothing more than a promise.

'We haven't got a tower,' Sophie said. She was picking at her fingernails.

Caro took a drink. She wasn't having that argument again. Two hundred dollars – at least – to put the monstrosity up, and even then there was no guarantee you could watch the Adelaide stations without snow. It's not like they'd be missing much. Anyway, Sophie watched too much television. Caro leaned further back. She tried to keep her yawn small.

'I've never seen black nail polish before.' It was Heidi. She had a drink in one hand, Zac awkwardly on her lap. 'It's different, isn't it?'

Right here, right now, Caro could fall asleep.

'They won't let you wear that at school,' Heidi said.

Sophie was picking at her fingernails. Caro wanted to say 'don't pick', but how many times had she said it and nothing had changed? She wanted to slap at Sophie's hands.

'There's white,' Heidi said. 'I used to wear white to school. You're not allowed to wear coloured polish, but they never notice white. If they catch you, you can tell them white's not a colour. The school rules say no coloured polish on fingernails, but white's not a colour. They teach you that in art.'

'If white's not a colour then neither is black,' Sophie said.

'That's true.' Heidi laughed, but then she looked at Caro and bit at her lip. 'But they'd notice it. And there's clear. Aren't you allowed to wear clear in year eleven and twelve? I've probably got a spare bottle of clear you could have.'

Sophie, her arm stretched out, was peering at her hands.

She looks like my mother, Caro thought and the snatch of memory lingered, although Caro had never seen her mother caring about her nails. She had no memory of emery boards or half-used bottles of polish among the drawers her father had asked her to empty. No cuticle sticks or clippers or even scissors. No cream or potion. It must be something in the way Sophie was holding her arm, or perhaps the tilt of her head. Nothing at all to do with hands or fingernails. Perhaps.

'White might work,' Sophie said, stealing a glance at Caro and flicking her hair before she looked at Heidi again. 'We weren't allowed to wear black at my old school either, but Caitlin and I still did.'

Caro knew she should say something, but she was too tired to argue about nail polish again.

She took a small sip of warm white wine. She couldn't wait to get into bed. And it was too soon to ask Joel for another cigarette.

CHAPTER FOUR

It was Mrs Robbins behind the desk, and there was no one else in the waiting room.

No one.

None of the other girls who worked behind the desk.

No one waiting for a doctor.

No one?

Heidi stood in front of the counter, holding Zac's hand.

'I've got an appointment with Doctor Riley.' She was annoyed at the crack in her voice. 'Caro.'

Mrs Robbins looked from Heidi to Zac to Heidi again.

'For you or for Zac?' she asked. She clicked the end of the biro up and down.

Stop that clicking, Heidi wanted to say.

'I need to know which notes to get,' Mrs Robbins said, and clicked the biro again.

Her roots are showing, Heidi thought. Her roots are showing and underneath the red she is going grey.

'For Zac,' Heidi said.

She shifted her eyes to the appointment book as Mrs Robbins crossed off their names. Who else is in there, Heidi wondered, and when are they coming? But the lines were thin and from where she stood, the book was upside down.

'Take a seat. Doctor Riley – Caro – got called to a home visit, but she won't be long.'

Heidi turned and went to a seat, sat with Zac in her lap, but he slid off and went to the box of toys in the corner of the room.

The phone rang.

'Would Tuesday at eleven suit . . . Doctor Clarke. All right, we'll see you then, Missus Johnson.' A click of the phone as Mrs Robbins put it down.

Why was the waiting room empty?

Even the radio was quiet.

She shouldn't have come. There was nothing wrong with Zac. She should just ring Mum, get it over with. Tell Mum: I'm engaged and I didn't take Zac to the doctor after all, because I think he's just short and pale, that doesn't mean he's sick. And then she would end: No, I didn't take him to see Mr Robbins. No, I'm not going to. No.

Mum doesn't know anything, and it doesn't matter what she thinks.

Heidi did not look Mrs Robbins' way, but she knew the woman had moved into the waiting area now, that she was picking up cushions and fluffing them, then putting them back on the chairs, that she was shifting the pamphlets in the stand, straightening the magazines.

'How was Queensland?' Mrs Robbins asked.

Like she didn't know. Like she hadn't tried to ruin everything.

Heidi had watched when Mum answered the phone, but she hadn't taken much notice until she realised Mum was saying things like, Yes of course I know who you are, and, Oh, I do remember that, and, Yes, I see, of course I'll talk to her. And even then it wasn't really the words that gave it away, but more the way Mum turned her back on Heidi and twisted the phone cord in her hand.

Heidi's mouth and throat felt dry.

She still didn't know how Mrs Robbins had got Mum's phone number because Heidi was supposed to be the only one who had it and she had only given it to Renee. How did Mrs Robbins get it, how did she dare to ring, and how did she dare to say those things?

Until Mrs Robbins rang, Heidi and Mum had worked out a way to ignore the space between them, however heavy and large. They had silently agreed to edge around the missing years, to start their time from here. They had not asked each other questions or looked for explanations, but instead they had spent their days marvelling at their matching tans. They had shopped for bags and shoes, letting shopkeepers call them sisters, they had filed each other's nails, swapping silver polish for pink.

They had let themselves believe they did not need any more and they had nearly proved that you could build a bridge with Pimm's and lemonade.

But then the phone call came and Mum had started to say, You should let them see Zac, he hasn't got much time. Like she had any right to say or even care. In the end, Heidi had told Mum, You have to be on my side, and if you're not, I'll leave. She left, I'll ring Dad, unsaid.

Now, Heidi could feel Mrs Robbins wandering round the room, but she told herself, I will not speak and I will not look around.

I will not speak.

I will not look around.

'Brad's coming home for a few weeks,' Mrs Robbins said. 'He's got two weeks holiday. You could come for tea. You and Zac. I could do roast chicken and Yorkshire pudding.'

Heidi kept her breath as light as she could.

She could stop herself from speaking, she could stop herself from looking. But she could not stop the thoughts: Do you still have the green chairs? Would we use the plates with the crazy glaze? Will we have Turkish coffee with dessert?

Heidi's mind was filled with the thoughts of Sunday nights and homework not quite done. Gravy made with chicken fat. *Countdown* on. Wiping dishes while Mrs Robbins washed. Mrs Robbins didn't use a dish rack and it meant that nothing drained and the towels soaked with water that wrinkled her fingertips. No one wore shoes in the house, and at the sink they stood on a straw mat which was one big square made of sixteen smaller squares. The straw was smooth on your skin, and slippery when you wore socks.

Brad was in the background. 'We should go and finish our maths,' he said, and offered her sly winks. But Mrs Robbins was asking questions about their English texts – *To Kill a Mockingbird*, *The Old Man and the Sea*, *The Summer of the*

Seventeenth Doll – so Heidi stayed to wipe the glasses, plates, crockery and pans.

One night after the washing was finished, but the putting away was not, Mrs Robbins said, I wanted to be an English teacher, you know, and that made Heidi think. An English teacher. That could happen. That wouldn't be impossible. So Heidi said, me too, and Mrs Robbins said, you should call me Vicki.

Heidi closed her eyes for a moment.

I will not look.

I will not be tricked by the smell of lemonfresh liquid and the sounds of cupboard doors.

Mrs Robbins was almost at Zac now.

'And I bet you started school, did you, Zac?'

Five years of silence had been more simple than this. You knew where you stood with silence. Nowhere.

Zac nodded.

'And who's your teacher?'

'Missus Trezise.'

'Is she nice?'

Zac nodded again, then furrowed his brow for a moment before he looked away.

'It's hard for the mums though, isn't it? When your baby starts school.' Mrs Robbins kept talking. 'I remember when you lot started school. You and Renee and Brad. We stood at the gates, all us mums, pretending not to cry. And your mum was the worst of them all. Because she only had you, I think.'

Heidi did not speak. She did not look. She would not let

Mrs Robbins know about the lump in her throat that took two weeks to go. Or the ache in her arms which started at nine in the morning and ended at three in the afternoon.

Heidi leaned across to the magazines, spread the pile across the table then picked out one from the bottom. She opened the magazine with no intention of reading it.

Just shut up. Why don't you just do your job. Why don't you just shut up and leave me and Zac alone.

'How's he going? Is he loving it?'

'He's fine.'

She had spoken. Shit. She had been tricked. It was because of wanting to be one of those mothers who said, Oh, yes, he loves it, he was really ready for it. He was getting so bored at home. I go to pick him up, and then he never wants to leave; when Zac wasn't one of those children and Heidi wasn't one of those mums. That's how she'd got tricked.

'It does take some of us a while,' Mrs Robbins said. 'Like Brad. It took Brad a while.' There was a small silence. 'But I bet Zac is like you in the end,' she said. 'I bet he's gonna be the smartest one in the school.'

Zac dropped a car on the parquetry square. The noise shot through Heidi's head. She looked at Zac.

From the side like that, he really looked like Brad. Something about the cheeks, Heidi thought. Or maybe it was the nose. Whatever it was, he looked like Brad. Heidi rubbed her hands over her face, then held them tight against it. Her eyes were closed and her breaths felt warm. She opened her eyes, but kept her hands against her face. She liked the orange light that came through her fingers. It reminded her of the days when she was just a little girl, and nothing had gone wrong.

Where was everyone? Why wasn't there anyone else?

When would Caro come?

'So what do you think about this weekend? Do you think you'll come?'

Fuck this, Heidi thought. Fuck Brad's dad. Fuck Zac being pale. Fuck Brad. Fuck Mum.

'Come on, Zac,' she said. 'We're going.'

As she pushed on the door, she felt for the weight to lift. For her chest to open up. For her breaths to be free.

None of these happened. But still, she couldn't go back.

CHAPTER FIVE

Caro was looking forward to a cigarette and a gin. The day had dragged. Conjunctivis, chicken pox and colds. And now, before she went home, she had to try and fix this mess with Heidi.

She held her hands on the back of her neck, let her head fall back.

Heidi. It was complicating her life. Complicating it all round. At work. With Libby. Of all the things she had imagined, talked herself through, this mess was not one of them.

She looked at the clock. Half an hour more, then she could have a cigarette.

She went to the waiting room and called Heidi and Zac.

'Say hello to Aunty Caro,' Heidi said.

Aunty. She was sure, if she'd been asked, she would have said just call me Caro . . . please.

'Hello, Aunty Caro,' Zac spoke automatically. The way children did when you told them to speak. Say thank you. Thank you. Say please. Please.

'Hello, Zac,' Caro said. Even to herself she sounded awkward and forced. She led them down the short corridor listening to the click of her heels and the shuffle of Heidi's shoes. She held the door while Heidi walked Zac in. None of them said anything as Heidi took the patient's seat at the side of the desk and Caro went to hers.

She had rearranged the furniture that morning, shifting the desk so she could catch the view of the courtyard from her seat. Not that it was much to look at: a dry and dusty square with cut-back ferns in pots. 'You cut them back to help them grow,' Vicki Robbins had told her. When she first moved into the room, Caro had her back to the window, but it seemed that if you had a window, you should be looking out of it. It would have been a nice window once. Before they'd put that false wall in and made two rooms out of one and the window became a sliver shared between two rooms and given strange proportions.

It was the third time she had rearranged the furniture and there wasn't much else she could try, but the room still wasn't working. With the light like that, Caro couldn't see the patient's face clearly. And the distance between them was wrong. She turned on the lamp. That was better, at least she could see Heidi's face, but the light like that made the room too clinical, too much like an inquisition. She would have to put the desk back to where it was yesterday, even if it did mean wedging herself between the desk and the wall. Even if it meant no view of the courtyard at all.

She should have painted the room, Caro thought, like she had planned to do. On her first day, sitting at her desk and looking around, she had thought then of painting it white. Silo white. But then she had unpacked the boxes one by one. Photographs, prints on the walls, models of muscles and bones. Her Mont Blanc pen and an emery board. And by that night, everything was out of the boxes, put away, her old office reconstructed here. The time for painting had passed. She would have to get used to moss-green walls with forest green for contrast.

Caro leafed through the notes, not looking for anything, just buying time, wishing she had planned more carefully what she was going to say.

She caught another waft of the roses. They had been doing that all day, wafting in and around, so that however hard she tried to push him away, they made her think of Graeme.

She had been taken by surprise when Vicki Robbins brought them in. You've got roses, she had said. There's a card, she had added, as she handed it to Caro still in its envelope. As Caro took the flowers and the card and said thank you, she had thought, for a moment, of telling Vicki Robbins. Caro thought of telling her, this woman she had only just met and barely knew, and of asking, So what would you do? But it had only lasted a second or two, as she remembered the energy you needed to have a friend, so Caro let Vicki stand for a moment too long in the door before Vicki had no choice but to say, Well, that's all, before she turned and left Caro's office and clicked the door closed.

Graeme had never sent flowers before – there had been no gifts between them, not since the earrings, and she had never given him a thing – but she had not needed the card to know who the roses were from. But she didn't know what they meant.

Even going over the words they had said on the phone she couldn't work it out. They could mean sorry or I miss you or goodbye, because in the end she had pushed him to say, I will get over you, if that's what you make me do.

His voice was soft and it bruised her soul.

I hope you do, she had said and rubbed at her nose so she wouldn't need to sniff.

He said, I know that you don't mean that, and she had sat silently, listening to the buzz of the phone. She was sitting on the floor by then, her back growing cold against the wall even while her ear was sweating against the receiver.

She ached in the spaces he could fill, but still she pushed him to it. She pushed him to say it again. I will get over you.

And then she had gone to bed to dream of snakes and storms and of rooms she needed to pack and of cardboard boxes endlessly unfilled. Between her dreams, she woke and thought of ringing him back, practising the words that she would never say, dreaming of breaking promises she was yet to make.

Caro shook her head now, trying to clear away the night before and the thoughts she'd had of his finger rubbing her cheek.

She made herself look more carefully at the notes before she looked to Heidi again.

Sitting together like that, Heidi and Zac looked a lot the same. If you looked past Heidi's black eyeliner rings, and the blush in aggressive streaks, if you looked past the lipstick and the foundation, there was something in the eyes that made them mother and child. The eyes, the shape of the face. But definitely not the nose.

The boy had wide blue eyes and thick blond curls. He

wore a creaseless shirt and pants. His socks were paired, and his shoes polished brown. These were the kind of details that Libby should like in a daughter-in-law. Caro remembered the days when Sophie would come home from holidays with white lace socks and hankies not just ironed, but ironed in triangles, not squares. Libby would ring after Sophie got home saying, She doesn't seem to have any socks, so I bought some new ones, I hope you don't mind. And Caro would yell at Sean and he would shrug and say, It doesn't matter, just ignore it, why do you care, and Caro would sleep on her side and refuse to speak with Sean.

Get it over with, she thought. Just begin. And don't yawn.

'I've heard about the other day when you came in.' Not a good start. 'I'm aware of the complexities in your relationship with Vicki Robbins.' Complexities? God, that was an understatement if even half of what Vicki said was true. 'First of all, I do want to reassure you that there are strict protocols about potential conflicts between our patients and our staff and, as a senior member of our staff, Vicki is well aware of those protocols.'

Heidi's look was blank.

'So while it may be uncomfortable for you in our reception area, it would be a conflict for her to handle your records.'

Still Heidi gave nothing away.

'Do you understand what I'm saying?'

Heidi shrugged and gave a nod.

'Good,' Caro said. 'So, how can I help you?'

Her leg twitched. She took another quick look at the clock.

'I don't know . . . it seems silly now . . . I mean, it was Mum's idea to see a doctor, and then when I met you, I thought you wouldn't . . . it's just . . . Mum was thinking there might be something wrong.' She kissed the back of the boy's head again, then mouthed the words, With Zac.

Zac was perched awkwardly on Heidi's lap. He was probably small for his age, but even so, he was big on her lap.

Caro looked at the notes again, but she was thinking of a cigarette. Remember when teachers could smoke in staffrooms and doctors could smoke in their rooms? They were Graeme's words, said as they lay together blowing smoke at the stars. A blanket under their backs and the smell of fresh-cut lawns. One cigarette. Two. Just one more, before she crept into the dark house, cleaned her teeth, crawled into the bed where Sean was pretending to sleep.

Caro stood up too quickly from her desk and her pen fell to the floor. She moved the flowers to the window sill and opened the window.

'Excuse me,' she said to Heidi. 'They're giving me hay fever.' She rubbed at her nose and pretended to sniff.

'You know,' Heidi said, she was craning her neck to see past the flowers and into the courtyard, 'If you burnt those ferns down they'd grow back much stronger. Cutting them back does work, but burning ferns is better. And it's kind of fun. Burning ferns.'

Caro looked for a moment at the cut-back ferns in their dusty pots. Burning couldn't make them look any worse. 'I'll pass that message on,' she said. She sat and shuffled further back through the file, making herself concentrate as she read. Nothing out of the ordinary. Bouts of vomiting, diarrhoea, colds, fevers, ear infections, a virus every now and then. Nothing unusual at this age. He'd missed last year's whooping cough that everyone was still talking about.

'What are some of the symptoms? What makes you – or your mother – think that there's something wrong?'

'He runs out of energy really easily. Everyone says he's placid, but sometimes it seems like he's just too tired to move.'

'Anything else?'

'He's pale. And he's really, really small. Much smaller than anyone else his age.'

'Right.' As vague as that? Without looking at the clock, she went through the motions. Weighed him. Measured. Checked eyes, ears, throat. Deep breaths in. And out. In. Out again. Went down the list: language skills, coordination, diet, counting. Nothing out of the ordinary. She smiled when she thought she should, made reassuring sounds. Zac cooperated. Like most other kids his age, he was uncertain, but he did what she asked.

Caro tried not to, but she was still thinking of a gin.

'Zac would you like to do some drawing?' she asked. She needed to try and talk to Heidi without Zac listening. Anyone else and she would have sent him out to play with the toys in the waiting room, but obviously that wasn't an option here. She gave him textas, paper and post-it notes and cleared him a space on the coffee table. It would have to do.

Sitting back in her seat, she got straight to the point.

'And how is life for you at the moment?' she asked.

'What do you mean?' Heidi's voice was sharp.

Shit. Why had she started this? Why didn't she just apologise for Vicki, ask some perfunctory questions, and then let it go. There was nothing wrong with the boy.

'Just are you generally happy, is there any stress? That kind of thing.'

'You've seen how life is,' Heidi said. 'It's good. I've just been to Queensland. I've just got engaged. Life is good for me.'

Heidi's hands were clenched on her lap. The skin looked tight, the knuckles white.

'Even happy events – like an engagement – can be a source of stress. You know, wanting everything to go right, trying to please everyone. And I understand your trip to Queensland might have been difficult at times.' Might have been – what was that supposed to mean. 'Perhaps that was affecting Zac. Children pick up on our anxieties and tensions much more easily than we realise.'

'I'm not tense. Or stressed.'

'How does Joel get on with Zac?' Caro asked.

'Joel loves Zac. You saw him the other night. He's great with Zac. He wants three more children. So altogether, we'll have four.' Heidi unclasped her hands, scratched her fingers through her head.

Sean had wanted four children too, and Caro thought of Libby, every year at Christmas saying, I always thought I would have more children. I didn't plan that gap between my boys. Always adding question marks that Caro still ignored. 'I meant does Joel think there's anything wrong with Zac?'

'I haven't asked him.'

Caro picked up her pen again, tapped it on the table, looked down at the notes she had been scribbling.

'You said it was your mother who thought you should bring Zac in for a checkup?'

Heidi nodded.

'And what about you, what do you think?'

'Me?'

Caro nodded.

'I think he's small,' Heidi said. 'I think he's small and he's pale and in winter he's always sick.'

Caro thought of the Christmas Days to come. Joel at the head of the table, Libby at his right, Heidi at his left, and her at the other end. She thought of the wondering she would have to do: what do you buy a twelve-year-old boy, a four-year-old girl. She thought of Libby's silent question marks and of the toast to absent friends.

A cigarette and a gin.

'I haven't found anything remarkable,' she said. 'But there are a few tests I might do, just to eliminate possibilities and reassure you.'

'What kind of tests?'

It was easier not to give too many names to things. Names led to questions that probably never needed to be asked.

'Just a few simple blood tests to make sure there's nothing there that shouldn't be.'

Caro wrote out the orders for bloods, thinking all the while about a cigarette and a glass of gin. Maybe two of each.

CHAPTER SIX

Heidi wrote 'INVITATIONS' across the top of the first sheet. She used small, even capitals and she was really pleased with the 'S'. Underlining the whole word twice, she looked at it, her head on the side. The second line wasn't quite straight, but there was no point starting again. If it wasn't the line, it would be something else. The 'A' would be too tall or the 'O' would be too wide.

She wrote the numbers down the side, a full stop after each one. There were thirty-eight lines. Thirty-eight was okay: five netball teams or two footy teams, more or less. Thirty-eight was the classroom in the morning when all the mums were saying their goodbyes. She could cope with thirty-eight.

'So who do you want to invite?' she asked Joel.

'Can we have a beer first?' he asked.

He was standing with his back to the sink, arms folded across his chest. He smelt of the shower and his hair was still wet and heavy with the water. It looked more straight, more dark, longer than it really was. He hadn't shaved, and he was wearing the afternoon-blue shirt, the top three buttons undone so she could see he was wearing his pendant again, a

Sagittarius symbol on a silver box chain. The first real present she had given him.

Had he taken it off before she left, or while she was away? She wondered where he had been keeping it, because she hadn't given him the box.

He wanted to start with a beer, but it was eight-thirty and she had told him to be here by eight. Yes, I promise, Joel had said and she watched him write it on his hand. 'Heidi 8'. He did not say sorry when he arrived at twenty-five past.

The party wasn't even her idea but Libby had said, Everyone has a party when they get engaged. Caro and Sean had a lovely party, didn't you, Caro? Everyone came. Heidi liked the way that Caro had looked at Libby and said, A party? I don't know, it was so long ago.

Course we're having a party. That was Joel. We'll go the whole hog. Engagement, buck's night, wedding, honeymoon . . . you only get married once.

'Not yet,' Heidi said. 'No beer. Just sit down and think. Who do you want to invite?'

'I dunno. Just the usual. Rick, Shep, Johnno.' Joel reeled off names as he walked to the fridge, and Heidi wrote them all, then added extra names. Kim, Flip, Sharon. Girlfriends, fiancées and wives. Everyone came in pairs. And if everyone came in pairs, then thirty-eight meant seventy-six, more or less, and there was nothing small about that.

She sighed again. Loud enough to be heard.

Joel opened the fridge, bent down to look. 'This all you

got?' he asked. He sniffed. 'I should have brought some more around.'

He should have too, because Dad had bought a bar fridge on the cheap from Ross, and now he kept his beers in the shed. Dad hadn't said anything, not to Heidi or to Joel, just bought the fridge and moved his beers outside. That's the thing about your dad, Auntie Barb always said. It's not his way to complain.

Joel lifted the bottle in a question mark, but when Heidi didn't answer he spoke.

'Beer? Yes or no?' He dipped his head into the fridge again. 'There's lemonade. I could make you a shandy. Do you want a shandy?' He stood up and looked at her now.

'No,' she said, her voice short and sharp. 'Anyone else? Do you want to invite anyone else?'

'Are you okay?' he said. 'You seem a bit worked up.'

'Yeah, course I'm okay. I just want to get this done. Your mum rang me today, and she wants to know. So it would be good if we could just finish this list. Who else?'

'Jamie, Corey, Duane.'

'Is Duane still going out with Rosanna?' Heidi asked.

'Dunno, yeah, think so.'

Heidi put an asterisk next to Duane, wrote Rosanna on a separate line. She would have to check. She closed her eyes, and it was hard to force them open again. She could hear the beer fizz as he opened the bottle.

'Liam, Marco, Chris, Gav, Walrus, Cass . . .'

She opened her eyes, kept writing names.

'Foster, Jimbo, Hughie, Roy . . .'

Heidi had reached the bottom of the page.

'Bennie, Declan, George . . .'

There would have to be speeches and she would have to stand at the front of the room, and people would be watching when they cut a cake.

'Simmo, Lester, Brownie, Jack . . .'

If Simmo and Lester came, then so would Mandy and Sal, and they would smirk at her and whisper behind her back and she would pretend she didn't hear, but they would know she did. They would wear clothes they had bought in Adelaide and show diamonds that were bigger than hers.

She drew a line down the middle of the page, and went back to the top, starting another column. Kept adding the bloody names.

'Lewis, Rocky, Digger, Frank . . . That's about it, I reckon . . . oh, no, there's Brett, Jason, Ian, Greg . . .'

Heidi put down her biro.

'I was thinking maybe let's try to keep it small. Perhaps just family. Immediate family. Close friends at the most.'

'Why?' he said, reaching for the packet of cigarettes in his shirt. She pushed the ashtray across the table, the one she'd emptied half an hour ago.

'I dunno. I just want to keep it special. Just for us.'

'Shit, I nearly forgot.' A folded piece of paper came out with the cigarettes. 'This is who Mum wants.' He pushed the piece of paper across the table to Heidi.

'All these?' Heidi spoke before she could stop herself.

Another whole page, filled with people she didn't even know. 'At the engagement?'

Joel shrugged. 'It's just the family,' he said. 'Cousins and shit.'

Heidi put Libby's list on the table in front of her, held it with her left hand, smoothed it with her right. She'd let it sit for a day or two, think of what she was going to say, the words she was going to use. They didn't have to talk about it now.

She reached across the table, took Joel's hand, put his finger in her mouth. Pulled it out, used it to trace the outline of her lips, dropped her head and gave a long, slow blink. He smiled back, got out of his chair, kissed her lips lightly once, then twice. She used her tongue and heard him groan.

She would sort out the invitations tomorrow.

CHAPTER SEVEN

'He's early.' Heidi looked at her watch. 'There's still ten minutes to go.' She rubbed at her throat then scratched at her head with both hands

'It'll be okay,' Caro said, but even as she spoke she was remembering, as she had a hundred times during the night, the paediatrician bellowing at her down the phone, making her blush and sweat in ways she hadn't done since she was an intern. I'm writing to the minister, he'd said. The letter will be on his desk this afternoon. What kind of show are you running up there? You've got children with unacceptable – not just unacceptable, dangerous – blood lead levels and even the doctors can't see it.

She'd tested for everything. Gone as far as leukemia. And it was only because the paediatrician was here for his monthly rounds, and because it would get Heidi off her back, that she had sent Zac along. By then she had crossed every 't' and dotted every 'i'. She had tested her instincts by looking in textbooks that hadn't been opened for years. At the surgery meeting, she had checked with Evan and Steve. Can you think of anything I could have missed?

But even though she'd read that CSIRO report last year,

and even though there was a thumping great smelting plant at the end of the street (had she really sat there and called it serene?), still she hadn't thought to test Zac's blood for lead.

It wasn't the paediatrician's job to talk with Heidi. It was hers. It was her job to sit across from Heidi and say, We need to get someone to look at your house because that's where Zac spends most of his time.

So he really is sick? Heidi had asked.

Yes, Caro had said, and bitten back the words, Isn't that what you want after a month of sitting in front of me shaking your head and demanding a second opinion?

When they visit, will you be there? Heidi had asked, shifting in her seat and scratching at her fingernails. What could Caro say but yes?

Another knock.

'Would you like me to get it?' Caro asked.

'No. I'll go,' Heidi said.

The health inspector's name, Philip Crosby, was printed on a badge and pinned to his chest. Farah trousers, short-sleeved shirt with a tie, biro in his pocket, pager on his belt. Brown shoes with pinholes in the toes. He shook Caro's hand.

'You the new lady doctor? I've been meaning to come and make myself known to you.'

'Would you like a cup of tea?' Heidi asked. 'And a biscuit?'

'Thanks, that'd be nice. Black and two,' Philip Crosby said. He opened a black folder, took the pen from his pocket.

'We'll start with your full name,' he said. '. . . and still just

you and your old man the only adults living in the house . . .
just the one child . . . and his full name . . .' He paused for a
moment. 'And he hasn't started school?'

'He's just started. They have Wednesdays off for the whole
first term. To help them settle in.'

'Number of years resident in this house?'

Caro sipped at her cup of tea. She could do with a cigarette. 'Heidi made these,' she said, and pushed the biscuits to
the middle of the table.

'Can I have a biscuit?' Zac said.

'Please,' Heidi said.

'Please.' Zac repeated the word.

'Just one,' Heidi said.

'History of illness . . . former places of residence . . .' Philip
Crosby went on.

As Zac finished the biscuit, Heidi took a banana and gave it
to him.

'Your occupation . . . occupation of other adults . . .'

As Zac peeled, the banana broke and fell to the ground.
Heidi bent down, picked it up, gave it back to Zac.

Philip Crosby wrote something down.

'All right . . .' He looked up and smiled at Heidi. 'That's
that section finished, let's move on. How often do you dust the
house?' he asked.

'Um . . . I couldn't tell you exactly, but probably every
fortnight.'

'Perhaps not quite as often as you should, eh? My missus is
the same. Reckon youse are all like it.' He looked from Heidi

to Caro, then back to Heidi again. 'Do anything before you'd dust, wouldn't youse?'

'Wouldn't you?' Heidi asked.

'Vacuum?' he asked. 'Mop? All of the house? What about the bathroom? Carpets? Are they shampooed? Curtains? Are they regularly washed?'

Like a house could get this clean overnight, Caro thought.

'Right, we'll have a quick look round the house, then the yard.'

Philip Crosby followed Heidi through the door.

Caro had been on enough house calls now to know, without leaving the kitchen, that the house had three bedrooms, two of them especially small, a bathroom, separate toilet, and a linen press in the hall. She knew the door handles were silver and probably squeaked, the light switches were white and the bathroom walls were tiled.

'Hey!' An enormous black cat had jumped on to the bench. Caro hadn't heard it come in the room. 'Get down!' She spoke to it as quietly as she could. 'I'll bet you're not allowed up there.'

The cat didn't even look at her. It sniffed at the open carton of milk.

'He always gets up there,' Zac said.

Caro could hear them coming back down the hall.

'Get down,' she said again, but the bloody thing didn't even look. She picked it up, heavy in her arms, and fur rough against her hands. It wriggled away from her, scratching her on the way.

'Time for the garden,' Philip Crosby said. Caro followed them into the yard.

The lawn was thick and neatly mown. A clothes line stood in the middle of the lawn at the end of a concrete path. No clothes on the line, no pegs. A budgie in a cage, the cat. Vegetables here, flowers there. A shed, a greenhouse, a tightly coiled hose.

Zac went to the sandpit and started to dig, lifting the sand into the tray of a yellow Tonka truck.

'I see your dad's still got a couple of tomatoes,' Philip Crosby said, as he stepped over the chicken-wire fence of the vegetable garden.

'Don't touch anything,' Heidi said.

Philip Crosby stood with his hands on his hips. 'Cucumbers, zucchini, capsicum,' he said.

It made Caro wonder how Sean's garden was going now. When she rented out the house she had tried to choose the family that cared the most, that knew about gardens and keeping things alive. She had dropped the rent because it was a bit more than they could afford, but none of the others who came through had looked at the vegies and roses while their children rolled on the grass. It was the only family she could trust to prune the peach tree, to keep the soursobs down, to care that the bulbs came up.

On the day before she left Adelaide, she'd walked around and told the plants, You'll be better off with them than you ever will with me. Caro was not a gardener in the same way that she was not a cook, not a runner and not good with her hands. She liked to dream and talk of gardening, and in the days when time with Sean was better than time alone she had walked around the yard, waved her arms, and said to Sean, Why don't we do raised flower beds? We should plant a chamomile lawn. She liked to say 'jasmine' and 'wisteria vines'. She would have liked a folly. And fairy lights.

There were remnants still of all those dreams. She had seen them on that last walk around the house. The catnip Sean planted for the kitten that had long ago grown into a cat and died. The spearmint she had used for making cups of tea. The rusted wrought-iron garden seat, bought for the gazebo that Sean had never built.

Then she had noticed other things too. A bottle brush, a grevillea, a lemon-scented gum, their labels faded and pocked with holes. She remembered, as she looked, that he had talked of them. The bottle brush for colour, the grevillea to bring the birds, the gum for its scent when it rains. And then the red rose, the yellow rose, the white. How long had they been there? She couldn't remember him planting them.

Packing up, she had brought the pots of rosemary, oregano, thyme and, because they had survived the trip when the box of glasses had not, she put them at the back door, and in the mornings when she left for work she would break a leaf or two of each, roll them in her hands, breathe their crushed scents in and make herself think only thoughts of Sean.

'Does your dad ever do strawberries?' Philip Crosby asked.

Heidi nodded. 'But the birds always get 'em. Even with the nets.'

Philip Crosby took a step between the rows.

'You should get out of there,' Heidi said.

'You drink the rainwater?'

'Course,' Heidi said.

'What's in the shed?'

'Dad's furniture.'

'I thought he used Smith's warehouse for that.'

'They needed the space back.'

'D'you mind if we take a quick look?'

'You can't touch anything,' Heidi said, but Philip Crosby pulled the side door open, reached inside and a light came on. Caro was hit by the smell of lacquer and paint.

'Is Zac allowed to play in here?' he asked Heidi.

'When Dad's around. He's made him his own workbench.' She pointed. Philip Crosby scribbled notes.

'Well, I think that's everything,' he said.

He looked at Caro then. 'I'll do you up a bit of a report. I'll be recommending a few simple steps. Nothing she won't be able to handle. Keep the pets outside. Regular dusting. That kind of thing.'

He stopped and looked around.

'Here's something to bear in mind . . . there's parts of the town where there's what you might call historic earth. With some traces of historic lead. But there's been a lot done down at the smelters, a lot of work's gone into controlling emissions. There's individual factors to be considered.'

Caro wasn't sure who he was talking to.

'That's good, isn't it?' Heidi said quietly when Philip

Crosby disappeared around the wall. 'What he said about it being simple.'

Caro nodded.

'Would you like another cup of tea?' Heidi said. 'Or would you like a sandwich? You could stay for lunch if you like.'

'No, I'm fine thanks.'

'Right.'

'I mean thank you, and of course I'd like to, but I need to get back to work.' She looked at her watch. 'It's my first appointment soon.'

A cigarette, Caro thought. Why had she left them in the car?

'Oh, yeah,' Heidi said. She put her arm around Zac's shoulder.

Caro looked at them. Thin, but not gaunt, neither of them. And the girl was not that much younger than she herself had been when Sophie was born. But it was hard to remember being quite that young.

'I'll see you later then,' Heidi said.

Caro went back to the car and lit a smoke. How hard would it have been to say yes. To have a cup of tea and a sandwich before she went to work.

CHAPTER EIGHT

'I still don't see why you want to do work experience at a hairdresser's,' Caro said. 'I mean what can you possibly learn?' She looked in the open fridge. There was cheese at least. A good-sized block of cheddar, a taste of the blue vein, and one of those cheap rounds of camembert. And a lonely jar of tahini she'd brought with them when they moved, because surely tahini didn't go off. She could make hummus, she thought. Hummus didn't take long. But what was the chance of having a tin of chickpeas in the cupboard?

'Gee, I dunno,' Sophie said. 'To be a hairdresser?'

Caro had no idea what to do. Sophie had faked Caro's signature on the forms and said, Well, I knew you wouldn't sign it, when Caro found out and confronted her.

'I could still tell the school,' Caro said now, plucking the cheese and a jar of gherkins from the fridge, carrying them to the breakfast bar. 'It's illegal, you know, to sign someone else's name. It's fraud.'

She had already taken the tonic from the fridge, the ice from the freezer. She looked at the 'food' and the drinks spread across the breakfast bar. 'People go to jail for fraud,' she said.

She would pour a drink first.

'It's not too late to change,' Caro said. 'I rang the school yesterday to check.' At least she had thought of ringing them. Planned to ring them. Got the number from Vicki Robbins, kept it by her desk for the whole of the morning and most of the afternoon, before she had thrown it out.

'You could go to the newspaper. Or the television station. I met Madeline Wilson the other day, I'm sure she'd find you a place. Wouldn't that be interesting? And there's a law firm – they've only got two lawyers, but they make lots of court appearances and they'd probably take you along. Or the hospital . . . I could get someone at the hospital to find you something . . . you might see an operation.'

'I hate blood,' Sophie said, although she'd never said that before. 'And I don't want to be a doctor. I want to learn how to be a hair and make-up artist.'

'I thought you wanted to be an actress,' Caro said.

'It can't hurt to learn the related elements of your craft. The more you can make yourself useful, the more likely you can be around to get your break.'

'I don't know where you got this whole stage idea,' Caro said, although she did. It was from being so bloody good in that youth theatre production of *Macbeth*, then getting the lead in *The Glass Menagerie* last year. Her name in the paper, the radio interview, that's where she'd got the idea. 'It's fun, but it's not a career.'

Caro bent down, took the glass from the cupboard, put four small blocks of ice in it. She measured the gin. A double. Just one.

'You shouldn't frown so much,' Sophie said. 'You'll get worry lines and then you'll look old before your time.'

'Don't be silly.'

'Anyway, when's tea?' Sophie said.

'Another hour or so.'

'What are we having?'

'I haven't decided.'

'You haven't even thought about it, have you?'

'I've thought, but I haven't decided,' Caro said. She took a lemon from the fruit bowl. It was shrivelling, but didn't look too bad. 'Go and do your homework while you wait. Or my ironing. I'm planning to wear the black skirt-suit tomorrow.'

If Sean had made that joke then Sophie would have laughed.

'I'm starving,' Sophie said. 'I can't do homework while my stomach's eating itself.'

Caro stopped herself from saying a stomach can't eat itself. 'Here,' she said. 'You can have this.' She took a plate, filled it with cheese and biscuits, a pickled onion and some olives. It had seemed the fridge was empty, but that didn't look too bad, Caro thought, as she passed the plate to Sophie.

Sophie looked down at the plate. She went to the fridge and took an apple.

Caro watched her walk away. It hadn't helped. Moving here. Taking an easier job. Being around. Even after a few months of getting home by five every night, Sophie hadn't noticed. She hadn't noticed any of it. The clean sheets, weekends at home, not even the odd banana cake.

Caro took her drink and the platter to the table, looked at the pile of journals and photocopied articles she had brought home. She took a drink, ate some cheese, tried to read.

It's just work experience, she told herself. It couldn't hurt. Look at those kids who used to come into the hospital for it. They weren't going to make a career out of it, were they? If anything, they were trying to eliminate careers. They were playing at being the people they didn't want to become.

Caro picked up the box of cigarettes that sat on the table. Only four left. She should have asked Sophie to pick up another packet on her way home from netball practice. She'd probably go now if Caro gave her a big enough note and let her keep the change.

Hairdressing. It was probably like the pony stage. Except I didn't have a pony stage, or a hairdressing stage. Or a debutante ball stage. That was the real decider, Caro thought. When Sophie had said, Mrs Woolf says I can help do the hair for the debs.

Debs? Caro thought it again now. Bloody hell.

She lifted a cigarette, tapped it on the box, put it between her lips, lit a match, then the cigarette. She waved the match up and down, but it didn't go out in time and she singed the tip of her thumb. She took a deep drag, then rolled the burning end around the top of the ashtray. This should be her last. She should stub it out. She should be a better example to Sophie. She took another drag. It was too late to give up today, but she could cook them some vegetables with tea. There must be something in the fridge.

It's ridiculous. Debutante balls. In this day and age. She blew gently at the top of the cigarette, watched the orange light slide around the tip, then took another drag.

Caro had tried making herself relax about it all. She stayed awake that night, made herself take a different point of view and told herself it was just a bit of fun. They all dress up and get their make-up done, their partners wear suits and bring the girls a corsage, and they have their photo in the paper. Gives them a chance to feel grown up and glamorous. It doesn't do any harm.

It hadn't worked. Because a debutante ball was girls in white dresses being led to altars by boys in suits. Another drag and another deep breath. She pressed her fingers against her forehead then took another drink.

Seeing Heidi today in her house like that was making it worse. The girl was obviously bright. Even Libby said it. All sorts of issues growing up, but she still managed to keep herself on track. Good grades, plans for uni, gets pregnant and that's the end of that.

You can't get pregnant cutting hair.

Was that Sean, that hollow voice giving that same answer every time. You can't get pregnant cutting hair. It was a man's voice. Deep. But were they really the kinds of words that Sean would use?

We shouldn't have moved. I shouldn't have brought Sophie here.

Caro tinkled ice against her glass. And then, unbidden, but loud, Graeme's words. But not his voice.

He will get over you, you know. If that's what you make him do.

Caro hadn't quite finished the cigarette, but she pushed the stub into the ashtray all the same, took another fag from the box, lit the match, then the cigarette, blew out the match, took a drag.

What were you and Graeme planning to do? Before you realised Sean was sick?

Who was that – who owned that voice? It could be Sean because he must have known about them. How could he not? She was his wife, Graeme his best friend. He must have known.

Caro took a final swig of her drink. They could have Chinese takeaway for tea. She looked at her watch. She'd better get it ordered. Everything closes at eight.

He will get over you, you know. If that's what you make him do.

Good, she made herself think it again, answering the voices in her head. I hope he does.

She took a drag on her cigarette, then pressed her forehead with her palm.

If they had Chinese, she would order lemon chicken and beef with cashew nuts.

CHAPTER NINE

When Mum first left, and everyone was saying Heidi couldn't live with Dad and they tried to make her live with Auntie Barb – it's not right, leaving it all to a man – Heidi made sure the house was clean and the clothes were always washed. She vacuumed and dusted every week.

After a while, when things had calmed down, and people were minding their own business again, Heidi had stopped dusting quite so often. She still did it, just not once a week.

But now, she started again. Now that the report had come, and they said it was her fault. The house wasn't clean enough, she needed to vacuum more, there was too much dust. Three pages of the flaws Philip Crosby had seen, the chores he thought she should do. Keep the cat outside. Keep Zac away from the shed. Don't let Zac eat the vegetables from the garden. Drink tapwater, don't drink water out of the rain-water tank. Mop the floors every day. Dust more. Vacuum. Don't let Zac eat dirt. Don't let Zac eat from the floor.

Is this gonna work? she had asked Caro, because it was different now that she knew Zac was sick. Things had changed. It wasn't just for Mum anymore, it wasn't just for making a point. Zac was sick. Her little boy.

Follow Philip Crosby's recommendations, Caro had said, twisting her fingers together while she talked, and even while she was worrying about Zac, Heidi couldn't help but notice – again – how beautiful Caro's hands were. Her fingers were long and her skin was still smooth. Her nails were never polished, but they were always shaped. Elegant. Just like her clothes, like the scarves in delicate fabrics, and the shirts in shades of cream. Come back in a couple of weeks and we'll test Zac again, Caro had said.

It wasn't an answer. It wasn't a Yes, this will work, or a No, probably not. But Heidi would do what she was told.

She made a routine.

Cleaning was easy when you had a routine.

She bought white index cards from the newsagent, wrote down the days of the week, the names of the rooms and the chores that had to be done, and filed them in the box. Every morning, she could look at the first card in the box, do what it told her to do, put that card to the back and look at the one in front to see what she should be doing next.

She had thought it was stupid when she'd seen it in a magazine all those years ago next to the hint about using a peg to mark the spot if you got interrupted when you were dusting the venetian blinds. Can't people even keep track of their dusting? she'd thought at the time. If you can't see where you're up to, then surely it doesn't need to be done. But now it seemed a good idea. Because this way, if anyone asked again, How often do you dust, she could always be sure. She could show them the cards and she could say, I dust every day.

She flicked through the cards now, although after two weeks she knew the order of the rooms and the chores. Zac's first. She always did Zac's room first. Just in case she didn't get through everything that day. If she did it first, it got done every day. Every single day. Everything did get done, of course. But just in case. She did the windowsill, the bedhead and the shelf. She dusted the top of the wardrobe every day, and used Marveer twice a week. Monday and Thursday one week, Tuesday and Friday the next.

Then vacuuming. She liked vacuuming now. Not like before when Zac was even smaller than now and always at home, and she had to hold him on her hip while she pushed the vacuum and he screamed in her ear the whole time. Now, she liked to watch the carpet underneath the vacuum as it got pushed back and forth. She like the sound of the dust and the grit going up the hose.

Thoughts started creeping in. Dad. Mum. Mrs Robbins.

She watched the vacuum going back and forth, but still the thoughts crept in.

After netball practice last night. Trying to get home in time to make Dad's tea. Zac on his bike while she walked, and then, Vicki Robbins blocking the footpath, her hands on her hips, the car stopped crooked on the side of the road.

Is he sick? Vicki Robbins had asked.

Heidi tried again to push the thoughts away. Watched the vacuum back and forth, back and forth. Caro had promised. No one else could look at Zac's records.

We've got a lawyer. We can take you to court, Vicki Robbins had said.

Fuck. A lawyer. The sound of the word still made her swallow then catch her breath. She couldn't afford a lawyer.

Just watch the carpet. Listen to the grit in the hose.

But the echo of Vicki Robbins' words wouldn't leave. We've got a right to see him. We're his grandparents. Brad's his father. We've got rights.

Vacuum under the bed and behind the chest of drawers.

Brad never came to see me, Heidi had finally answered back. Not once he knew. He never even spoke to me again.

Vicki Robbins had cleared her throat, opened her mouth as if to speak, closed it again, uncrossed her arms. They dangled awkwardly. She crossed them again.

I spoke to your mother again the other night. You know, I always liked your mum.

Mrs Robbins voice was as soft as her perfume which was violets or maybe geranium.

Everyone liked your mum, Mrs Robbins had said. And you're a lot like her.

No one had said that to Heidi before. No one except Mum.

I've never been to Queensland, Mrs Robbins had said. She had looked around, and Heidi followed her look. Down the road, straight and flat. It didn't really go anywhere that road. Just stretched until there was no more town. The sun was setting, a blazing orange ball. The air was still and quiet and smelt of sausages. Chops. Fried. Grilled.

I wonder what it would be like to live somewhere else, Mrs Robbins had said, and because of the way she still rubbed her finger under her chin, and because her voice was deep but light, Heidi had thought of telling Mrs Robbins about the cicadas, the rolling sea, the humidity. It's not like our air, she could have said. Our air is dry and it leaves a space between you and the sky. Dry air lets you breathe. But dampness closes you in and humidity fills your lungs.

Heidi shook her head. She had to get Mrs Robbins and her words out of her head. Out. Out. She turned the vacuum off and stood for a moment, taking deep breaths.

Had Mrs Robbins really rung Mum again? Because if she had, that meant Mum knew. About being engaged. About Zac. Mum knew and she hadn't rung.

Heidi moved to the bathroom. Began to mop the bathroom floor. Two buckets and two mops. One bucket and mop were for the Ajax, and one bucket and mop were for the plain water afterwards. She tipped the water down the laundry sink and did the breakfast dishes while she waited for the bathroom floor to dry. Then she wiped the bathroom floor with a towel to dry the last of it off. She took the towel straight to the laundry and put it in the laundry basket. The red was for wet towels, the blue was for dirty clothes, and the white was only for clean.

She planned what they would have for tea, what vegetables they'd use. The vegies in Dad's garden were still going strong, because there was no way she was going to tell Dad he had to stop his garden. She washed them under the tap, and she cooked them every night because if she didn't Dad would wonder what was wrong. But she didn't give them to Zac anymore. She only fed him what she'd bought from Scarletti's.

Back to the washing and trying not to think about Mum.

She had started to do two loads in the morning and one at night. The first was towels, the second was Zac's pyjamas, the third his clothes. She did not hang the clothes outside, but strung lines across the laundry and the bathroom, and she got up early to take down the bathroom clothes so they wouldn't get in Dad's way.

Dad's room next. He was on day shifts this week, so she could do it every day. It wouldn't be so easy when he was back on nights. Then, her own room. That was the easiest, took hardly any time. Vacuum and dust, it didn't need Marveer. Still left the lounge room and the kitchen to do, but that's fine, it's only half past twelve.

She made a cup of tea, a plate of biscuits with cheese, and took them to the lounge room.

She sat in Dad's chair. It still smelt like Dad and his after-work shower but it sagged more than she remembered.

She would have to tell Dad about Zac. Sometime soon. She would have to tell him the house has too much lead, it's making Zac sick. He would look at her in the way he always did. He might nod. He might shrug.

She thought of tipping the chair back and closing her eyes, but if she did that she might not open them again. She looked around the room at all there was to do. Perhaps she should pack the knick-knacks away. It would be so much easier to keep the dust down if she did. But she remembered how empty it felt when Mum first left, and Auntie Barb had taken all of Mum's statuettes, pictures, photos and souvenirs down.

They're just something to dust, after all, Auntie Barb had whispered as she carried the boxes away. Heidi wondered still what Auntie Barb had done with them all.

'Heidi? You home?' It was Renee, calling from the kitchen. Heidi hadn't heard the back door open or close.

'Heidi?' Renee was standing in the doorway of the lounge, Charlotte in her arms. Her hair was pulled back in a ponytail, and she had no make-up on, not even lipstick. Her eyes were bags, her skin was pale. Heidi stood up, walked over to peer at Charlotte.

'Oh, look at you, Charlotte,' she said softly, rubbing her finger against the baby's cheek. She took the baby from her friend. Heidi felt the heat of Renee's arm as they cradled the baby from one set of arms to the other. In her sleep, Charlotte's lips made tiny sucking moves.

The baby was warm against Heidi's chest. She was so light and her face was so small. Everyone says it, but you do forget. You forget how little they are. Heidi closed her eyes and it was easy to forget the baby would cry in the night and daytime too, and she might not sleep much. It didn't matter that she would need to be fed and her nappy would need to be changed. There was nothing that felt like this. This kind of warm.

You'd do anything for a baby, wouldn't you? You'd do anything to make sure everything was right.

Heidi opened her eyes, leaned her head into the child. She

left a kiss on Charlotte's forehead and then one on her cheek. She rubbed her hand up and down the baby's back.

There was nothing that felt like a baby against your chest.

She rocked the baby back and forth. She would do the lounge room next. As soon as Renee was gone.

CHAPTER TEN

Heidi did not stop to make another appointment. She walked straight past the waiting room and straight past the desk and she felt Vicki Robbins, felt them all looking and thinking, What's up with her, and she thought, Fuck you all.

She shook her head, and pushed the hair out of her eyes. What's the fucking point, you do everything they tell you, but it all just stays the same.

She took the few steps to the car. She turned the key, checked the mirrors and backed away from the kerb. Ignoring her seatbelt, she thought of driving until the town, Joel, Dad, Zac, Caro, everything was so far away that she couldn't touch it and it couldn't touch her. She would squeal the wheels and leave white smoke and black marks as she tore down the main street past Scarletti's and past the motel and over the railway line and she would never look back. She would not turn right for Adelaide and places known. Instead, she would turn left and drive with the Flinders on her right. She would drive, foot down, until she reached the desert and it was night, and she would get out of the car to lie on the bonnet, ticking and warm. The sky would be black and deep and she would count every single star. She would sleep beneath an open sky and her dreams would bring messages and tell her what to do, and when she woke her lungs would be clean, her bones would not ache, and her soul would be clear.

Instead, she drove at forty ks. Turned left at the service station. Right at the council chambers. Past the old customs house. Down onto the wharf.

There was one ship at the silos and one at the smelters' end. Heidi stopped the car under the silo cranes, got out, and leaned against the side of the car, the door still open.

The sickly smell of sulphur was heavy in the air.

The gangplank of the ship was down, but the gate was across and she couldn't see or hear anyone on board.

Kotte. Sri Lanka. The name of the ship, and its country of origin. They had learnt about country of origin in school, followed it up with an excursion to the wharf – permission slips, the yellow bus and the boys in the class pulling at themselves whenever Harold Smith talked about 'the tugs'.

It had been a Sri Lankan ship that night she'd followed Mum. Heidi had tried so hard, so often, to remember why she got out of bed that night. How had she woken and what had she known? There were no fights, no arguments, no shouts, no yells. But Heidi must have known not to sleep, because when she'd heard the back door creak, she had pulled on her cardigan, left the house, and followed Mum.

They were both on their bikes. Mum in front, a space, Heidi behind. Heidi had been as quiet as she could in the still night air. She watched for potholes that would make her mudguard rattle and used only her back brake because the front one squeaked. She followed Mum down South Terrace and Victoria Street, Main Street, the wharf. The moon was almost full.

On the wharf, Heidi's wheel got caught in the railway track and Heidi fell. Mum came back.

She held Heidi's face in her hands and looked into her eyes and said, Are you okay. Mum's fingers were cold on Heidi's cheeks, and her breath was warm and smelt of gin. Even at night, the smelters hummed.

What are they for? Heidi had asked, pointing to the large round silver disks rested on the thick ropes that tied the ships to the wharf.

They stop the rats from getting on board, Mum had replied.

Rats. And not only that, but with streaks of rust running in stripes down the sides of the ship, Heidi had worried for the sailors, imagining that in the high seas the holes would let the ocean in. Heidi pictured the night when the crew would abandon ship and the small orange boats would be lowered from their alcoves into chundering seas, and someone would shout, Women and children first, which meant that the captain's family would survive, but some of the men would die.

Three men dressed in white stood on the ship looking down. Mum had waved and Heidi had wanted to say, Mum! Don't do that! Don't wave.

The men had looked, but did not wave back, and Heidi had been glad.

They're Sri Lankans, Mum had said. They work for slave

wages. That was how Heidi knew that the reason they didn't wave back was because they were scared of the black-hearted captain who was watching them from somewhere up high. If they made contact with people on the land, they would be locked away with their rations halved, and they might even be thrown into the sea.

Heidi had dreamed of saving them, but she would be too scared to come back to the wharf at night. Especially now she knew about the rats.

They say there are beautiful beaches in Sri Lanka. And India too. They say that for five dollars a day you can live like a king, Mum had said. You can live on a kibbutz in Israel for twenty dollars a week or a squat in London for free.

When Mum left, Auntie Barb had said, It's one thing to run away, it's another to not even call and explain. Heidi had let herself believe that Mum had drowned on her way to Sri Lanka to live at the beach. Until finally Mum did call and she hadn't drowned. She'd been in Byron, Noosa, Darwin, Alice Springs. Mum called, but she never explained. She never explained a thing. Not Daniel or Sasha or why they weren't there when Heidi and Zac arrived. She didn't explain the house that sprawled with rooms that were never used. Mum didn't explain the dog that slept on her bed when she had always told Heidi dogs scared her. She didn't explain the diamond ring or the phone calls that came at eleven o'clock at night or three in the morning or four in the afternoon.

Heidi walked to the edge now, and looked down at the water that lapped black against the wharf and its barnacles. She watched the water lapping until it made her dizzy, then turned and took a step back to look across the creek, the mangroves, the saltbush flats, towards the Flinders Ranges. On the night she had been here with Mum, it had all been shadows and sillhouettes, but today the ranges stretched in shades of blue, their outline soft and barely defined against the sky. She remembered camping times. Magpies and crows, their calls in the mornings and in the afternoons. On walks with Mum, they had seen yackas, kangaroos and once a snake. Just leave it, it will go, Mum had said, as she took Heidi's hand. They had stood still together while the snake slid past. Noiselessly? Or had there been a rustle? Heidi could remember only the pounding of her heart.

Where was Dad when they camped? She had never thought about it before, but why was he never there?

Now Heidi could hear the hum of the smelters behind her, machines she had never seen. There was a furnace, she knew that, because Dad had told her, and because if you went to the end of the wharf you could sometimes see the flames. But she would never see it properly, never feel the heat that Dad and Joel described because, Girls don't work on the floor. That's all she'd learnt from that day in year ten, when the girls got marched out of the tech studies class, because the guy from the smelters was there to tell them about apprenticeships. Heidi had put her hand up and asked, Why can't we get apprenticeships, why can't we work on the floor? The man from the smelters had smiled, then said, Because girls have babies. Heidi was happy with the answer then, but now she wondered what he meant by that. Was it just because the girls would leave, or because it wasn't safe? And if it wasn't safe for girls, what made it safe for boys?

Heidi looked at the Flinders some more, tried to block out the noise from behind and to think of magpies and crows. It didn't work. She thought of the dusting that still had to be done today. She had mopped already and she had washed. But the dusting still had to be done.

She got back in the car, wound down the window, put the seat back, yawned, closed her eyes, let her body sink.

Her body grew heavy, but she did not sleep.

Mum had never dusted. It'll just be back tomorrow, she always said. And dusters just stir the dust up, better to let it rest. Heidi remembered that Mum said it where Auntie Barb could hear. And later, when Auntie Barb wasn't there, Mum had said, Let's dance in the dust, my love. They went to the kitchen window where the sun was coming in, and Mum blew on the windowsill and shook at the curtain, and then she showed Heidi how to rub at her hair to make the dust come out.

Together they had clapped at the dust and jumped in the air and laughed at Auntie Barb.

CHAPTER ELEVEN

Heidi carried Dad's tea in one hand, and Joel's in the other.

'Sorry there's no biscuits left,' she said.

She'd eaten the whole packet this afternoon. Started with just one, but that really meant two because biscuits have to come in pairs. One you eat on the left side, and one you eat on the right. Then she'd had two more. And again, until she couldn't stop and she'd finished the lot.

'I could do you a piece of toast,' she said. 'How 'bout jam and cream? There's enough cream there for a piece of bread or two.'

'It's fine,' Dad said. He was scratching Midnight between her ears. Two days now and they still hadn't said anything about the letter. Not really. And because they didn't ask, she couldn't explain: I did it because Zac is sick, because of the lead, and because Caro said the minister needed to hear it straight from the people it affected, and because Mum said it's what she would've done.

She shouldn't have sent it, she thought for the millionth time. Not on her own. She should've waited until there were others – there must be others – and written it then. She should've told Dad and Joel that's what she was going to do, should've known they'd be pissed off down in the smelters and take it out on Dad. Should've, would've, could've. They were Mum's words too.

She rested the cups on the mantelpiece then pulled out the two small tables. She moved the cups of tea to the tables. Dad's milky tea on one table, Joel's black tea on the other.

She hadn't thought it through. Not properly. She hadn't thought about their jobs and how it would be for them working there.

Heidi went back to the kitchen, put two spoons of sugar in her tea, stirred it quietly around. She took her cup, the sugar bowl and a dry teaspoon into the lounge, gave the sugar bowl and spoon to Dad.

'Thanks, love,' Dad said. He leaned forward reaching carefully over Midnight, put three large teaspoons of sugar in his cup.

Heidi watched. Milk in tea looked horrible, but she liked the sound of the spoon as he stirred it against the bottom then tapped it against the side. She wished he wouldn't leave the spoon on the table like that. Something else for her to clean. Isn't that what the saucer is for?

It was usually good this time of the night, when Zac was asleep, and there was nothing left to be done. With the telly on, she didn't have to worry anymore about whether Joel was annoying Dad, or Dad was annoying Joel. They could just sit together in peace.

But tonight, the peace was filled with words she didn't dare to say.

Four Corners was on. Boring as batshit, Heidi thought, but she didn't waste her breath complaining. Dad watched it every week, and he always had. He sat there, and he didn't say a word while he watched, and if you tried to speak he'd shush you down. Joel reckoned he liked it too, but Heidi wasn't sure.

Dad was leaning back, holding his cup with one hand and resting it on his chest.

He took a sip.

'Ahhh,' he said, the way he always did and sometimes strings of milk stretched between his lips. Heidi couldn't stop herself from looking to see whether the strings were there.

'Have you two thought about living together first?' Dad's question came from nowhere. He lifted the remote control, pointed it at the television, turned it down. Heidi could hardly hear. Shit. They were going to talk.

Dad put the remote on the arm of his chair. Heidi kept her eye on the telly, but she could feel that he was looking at her. She tried to stop herself, but she couldn't help looking his way again.

'You don't want to be talking to your old man about it, I know,' Dad said. 'And I try not to poke my nose in where it isn't wanted, you know that.'

Fuck, Heidi thought. At least he could've waited until Joel was gone. She looked away from Dad, as Joel cleared his throat, lifted his teacup and took a slurp.

She heard Dad shift in his chair, then sip at his tea.

'Getting married, it's a big decision. Especially for you, with a little one and all. There's Zac to think about.'

'We know that Dad,' Heidi said. She reached for her cup, held it in front with both of her hands.

'Don't get me wrong, Joel,' Dad said. 'You're real good with Zac, and I can see you love him. I can see that. But you don't know what it's like living with them all day, every day. It's a different thing, living with little ones. And when you're married . . . when you're with each other all the time . . . well, Heidi won't always be able to look after you as good as she does now. It's all right at the moment, when you're here just a few hours a day, and Zac is already in bed, because then she can do anything you want. But kids come first. They always do. Things'll change when you live together. Things change.'

Heidi could feel Joel sitting next to her. She wondered what he thought. What the fuck did he think about this?

'When Zac gets sick, or you have another little one and you're up all night again . . . it makes you tired, and she won't have the same time for you, Joel. She'll be tired and grumpy, and so will you, and goodness knows how little Zac will be. It's like I've said before. People don't know what they don't know.'

Dad went quiet before he spoke again.

'So I've got a bit of a solution. Youse could live here,' Dad said. 'For a while. Till Christmas maybe. Just for a while. It gives you a chance to find out what it's really like.'

'Joel's here nearly every day,' Heidi said. 'He has tea here nearly every night.'

'Yeah, but what's it like to wake up next to him every day? What's he like when he's in a bad mood? Will he mind when the weather's hot and you can't be bothered cooking and all you give him is a plate of tomato sandwiches?' Dad took another sip. 'I'm sure you see what I mean.'

He'd heard them. He'd heard them arguing. About the engagement party. Or worse.

I don't want another baby yet.

Why not?

I've just got Zac off to school.

And that's exactly why we should have one soon . . . there's too much space between them as it is.

I want to find a job.

And since the letter, Dad had probably noticed that Joel's goodbyes to her were just a kiss on the cheek and, I'll see myself out.

Heidi looked into her teacup. She looked at the tea-leaves sitting on the bottom. She was thinking of the house with Joel in it. She would cook his breakfast and pack his lunch and she would have his tea waiting when he came home.

She thought of Joel never going home and of always being here.

There would be no more staying up after Dad went to bed, just so they could be alone. No late-night trips to Joel's car, just so that Dad couldn't hear. No wondering where to go when the pub closed, but they didn't want to say goodbye.

No goodbyes.

She thought of Queensland nights and a hand on the back of her neck and one on her naked knee. What did it mean if you could still feel that way about someone else? Someone you didn't even know.

'There isn't room,' she said. 'His car doesn't fit in the drive.'

'We'll find the room,' Dad said. 'We can work that out.'

'What about Dog?' Joel said. 'The cat won't like Dog living here full-time.'

Dad nodded, rubbed Midnight along the length of her back.

'There's bits and pieces we'd need to work out, but I think maybe if you live together, it might help take the surprise out of things.'

Dad sat back in his chair looking somewhere, but Heidi wasn't sure where, and Dad was feeling something, but Heidi wasn't sure what. He took a gulp at his tea, then another.

Did he know what Mum had said? Did she say the same to him? It's easier to not get married than it is to get divorced . . . if you don't want a second baby, that doesn't mean that you don't love the first.

'So, the offer's there. You two have a think about it, and then you let me know.'

He put his cup down, pointed the remote at the telly again, and through the noise, Heidi thought of Queensland nights.

CHAPTER TWELVE

'I was really glad when you rang and booked yourself in. I've been wanting to have a proper talk with you. With Emma and Sophie being such good friends it isn't right that we've barely spoken before.' Suzie Woolf stood behind the chair and smiled at Caro in the mirror. Her lips were very red. 'But whenever I suggest anything, Emma has a blue fit. "Why don't we ask Sophie and her mother around for the barbecue," I said. You would have thought I'd said let's dance naked around a bonfire in the light of a full moon. Apparently, it would be far too embarrassing for you and I to meet. I'd be sure to say the wrong thing and then Emma would die apparently . . . She adores you, of course. Oh, yes, you must have known. If only you were her mother, she would be so much better off. She'd be able to buy her lunch nearly every day, she'd have seven pairs of jeans . . . you know the kind of thing. Because of course, all I do is lie in bed at night and plan ways to make her life a total misery.'

Caro half-listened to Suzie Woolf, while she wondered whether it would be possible to count the number of times she was reflected in the mirrors that lined the salon walls.

'And it was lucky really, because I don't usually cut on

Wednesday afternoons. It's ladies' day at the golf club. You should come along . . . I'll sign you in. Or Marj would do it, I'm sure. You must know Evan's wife? She's club champion.'

She had one hand each side of Caro's head, holding it gently still. Her own hair was swept into a smooth, silky bun which was streaked in shades of red. Her eyes were lashed and lined in black in classic fifties style. It looked good on Suzie Woolf.

'I've never played golf,' Caro said.

'That doesn't matter, it's not about the golf. You should come, you should come. Looks like you can clear your appointment book easily enough, and we need a few younger ladies.' She combed her fingers down the back of Caro's hair. 'We get a lot who start when their husband retires. You know the kind – I married him for better or worse, but not for lunch.' Caro knew from her laugh that Suzie Woolf had made the joke before. 'There's more to golf than meets the eye.' Suzie sighed. 'I miss my golf, but one of the girls – you might know her, Heidi's friend Renee? No? You'd know her if you saw her, I'm sure. Anyway, she's taken maternity leave and I haven't replaced her yet, and I just can't get away on any after-noon. We're so busy here.'

Caro counted the chairs without moving her head. With all these mirrors, she barely needed to move her eyes. She turned it into a test. How many can I see without moving my eyes? That wasn't easy. She had to move her eyes. The trick was to move them hardly at all then. Twelve. There were twelve chairs for customers.

'Maternity leave.' Suzie Woolf's voice dropped, she looked around, sat on the stool next to Caro's chair. 'I gave her a little extra when she left. Like a bonus, I mean. You know, just so she knows I value her. They'll have their eye on her down at Just a Trim. You mark my words, they'll be ringing her when the baby's a few months old, offering her a few hours here, a half-day there. Just whatever suits, whatever you can do, they'll say, and before you know it she'll be theirs.'

And how many hairdressers? Caro could see six women, all dressed in white, with blue trim and white shoes. Shaped and coloured hair. Did the girl sweeping the floor count? So seven if apprentices count. And there might be more for busy times like Christmas and Saturday mornings.

Suzie Woolf stood up. 'Course that's not something I'm telling everyone.'

She bent her head down so that her chin was almost resting on Caro's head.

'So, it's funny how things work out, isn't it? Both with Wednesday afternoons off, but here we are. Now, what are we going to do for you today?' She pushed her hands under Caro's hair, pulled it all to the back, put her hands on Caro's shoulders. The pressure of her hands was soft but her thumbs were strong and even through her shirt, Caro could feel Suzie Woolf's nails.

'Oh, just a trim,' Caro said. 'I really just want you to get rid of the split ends.'

'Well, I can do that,' Suzie Woolf said. She raked her fingers down the length of Caro's hair. 'Of course I can.

Although I must say,' – she gathered the hair and held it in a bunch with one hand, rubbed gently at the ends with the other – 'it's in very good condition already. There aren't a lot of split ends there. Perhaps . . . well have you thought about a change?'

Caro had not. 'I've had my hair like this since, well, for years,' she said, shaking her head as she spoke. 'It's always been like this.'

Always? No. Caro remembered skipping down a road, swishing long hair from side to side and watching her shadow's hair move. Plaits at school and playing the piano with clips to hold her hair behind her ears. Did it get shorter by degrees, or did she just go one day and ask to have it cut? Just kind of short with a fringe. And brown. It's how it had always been.

'Well, that's all the more reason for a change, don't you think? Nothing too dramatic, of course, but why don't we lift it off your face here? Look. You've got gorgeous cheekbones. They give your face the most wonderful shape and it would be easy just to enhance it if we cut the hair around here. And we could layer it a bit around the front and sides just here.' She chopped the sides of her fingers gently against Caro's face. 'Get rid of some of the weight. It will still be easy for you to do in the mornings. I won't leave you with anything you need to style.' She nodded. 'What do you think?'

'Okay,' Caro said.

'And a colour? I know you aren't booked in for one, but,' she lowered her voice, 'for you, I'll make the time. We've just started using a new range. Makes your hair look like glass.'

'I've never coloured my hair,' Caro said.

'Never?' Suzie's eyebrows lifted. 'Well, we won't do anything too radical. Again, just something to enhance. Let me get the chart and you can have a look.'

She returned with a book of hair samples held open across one arm. She let her finger caress each coloured knot, flicking it up then smoothing it down.

'This one's beautiful,' she said. 'A kind of chocolate brown.' She looked at Caro in the mirror again. 'It will really bring out the blue of your eyes.' She stopped. 'You know, you've got lovely eyes. I can see where Sophie gets hers from.'

Caro looked at herself in the mirror, but she couldn't see any lovely eyes. She saw a large, red nose and pale, dry lips. And she had never seen any of herself in Sophie.

Now would be a good time to bring it up, the work experience and the debs. Talking of Sophie, she could say.

'Well?' Suzie Woolf asked. 'What do you say?' Her smile was friendly and so were her eyes.

'Perhaps a change in style,' Caro said. 'But not a colour. Not today.'

'Well, okay, we'll leave the colour for today, but how about . . . well, I'll make sure you're not disappointed with the cut,' Suzie Woolf said. 'Then next time you come back maybe you'll trust me to colour it too.' She wrinkled her nose. 'We might even make the appointment when you leave today.'

'Perhaps,' Caro said.

'If you come over to the basin, I'll get Nadine to wash your hair.'

Caro followed Suzie Woolf to the basin.

'This is Nadine,' she said to Caro. It was the girl who had been sweeping the floor. She was taller even than Suzie Woolf. 'She'll wash your hair then bring you back to me.'

Nadine's hair was tied in a pile on the top of her head and she used the same fragrance Sophie sometimes used. If Caro were the type of person ever to say fragrance aloud, and if she were the kind of person to use finger quotation signs, she would wrap finger quotations around fragrance. Every time.

The seat Caro sat in was soft. Suzie Woolf and Nadine stood behind her and Suzie spoke in a low but demanding voice. 'Now what conditioner do you think we would use?'

Caro felt fingers on the top of her head. It must be Nadine picking up her hair and letting it fall, because Suzie's hands had been less tentative, more calm.

'How long since you washed your hair?' Nadine asked. Her tone made the question almost impolite.

'Ummm, I'm not sure. Yesterday, I think. Or maybe the day before,' Caro said. 'No, it was the day before.'

Nadine sniffed. 'Use the regular conditioner. The ends aren't dry, and there's only a bit of oil in the roots.'

'Good,' Suzie Woolf said. 'Now, just sit back and enjoy,' she said to Caro.

Nadine put a towel around the back of Caro's neck and tucked it in to the collar of her shirt. It felt bulky but unstable, as if Nadine had not pushed it in hard enough to make it stay.

'Lean back for me,' Nadine said. Her voice was not so soft now that Suzie had gone, but it was still flat. Caro leaned back. The basin was hard. She had to lift her chin and stretch her neck.

'How's that?' Nadine asked. 'Is that okay? Do you need to move your chair?'

'It's fine.'

Nadine turned the water on. The sound of the spray against the basin echoed. 'How's the water? Is that okay?' Nadine's hand was pushing the water into Caro's hair. You could press harder, Caro thought.

'Yes, thank you, it's fine.'

When Nadine held the nozzle close enough, the needles of warm water made it all the way to Caro's scalp. Knitting needles, Caro thought. She closed her eyes. Stretched like this, it was hard to breathe deeply enough. She yawned. It cricked her neck.

Nadine's bracelets clinked against each other, but thunked against the sink. She must be wearing a lot of them, Caro thought. Nadine turned off the water. Caro left her eyes closed. She heard the sound of the shampoo pump, felt Nadine rubbing the shampoo through her hair. Nadine's fingernails were long, but they did not scratch.

'It smells like peaches, don't you think?' Nadine said. More like nectarine, Caro thought.

'Yes,' Caro said, wishing her neck were not so stretched. She thought of going home after this. Of falling into afternoon-cool sheets, of the warm space her body would make in the bed. If she could make time for a haircut, surely she could make time for a sleep?

'Have you had a good day so far?' Nadine asked. 'Oh, yes,' Caro said. It would be polite to open her eyes, but she left them closed.

'Whatcha been doing?' Nadine asked.

'Oh, you know, just work,' Caro said.

'Oh, yeah,' Nadine said. She turned the water back on and rinsed Caro's hair. Caro wondered should she say something more, but she would have to shout to be heard over the water, and anyway, what would she say?

The water was off again.

'How about you?' she asked. 'How's your day been?'

'Not bad. I only just got in. I get Wednesday mornings off. I do the shopping for my Nan. It's too much for her now, and I do the shopping, because it gives Mum a bit of a break.'

A bottle squirted.

'We love her, but she's hard work. She's got dementia.'

It must be the conditioner now, the way Nadine was rubbing Caro's head in long and circular strokes. Nadine pressed her thumbs hard in behind Caro's ears then used the pads of her fingers to rub from the top of Caro's head around and down to her neck. Should she tell Nadine that it was much nicer this way, that she shouldn't start out pressing so soft?

'It doesn't get better. Dementia. You just have to remind yourself that she's not the real Nan,' Nadine said.

Caro was glad her eyes were closed.

Nadine had lifted Caro's head a little and was rubbing at the top of her neck. That was the place Sean had rubbed at the end of the day. When Sophie was in bed, when the lamp was on, the stereo playing, and the rest of the day stopped mattering.

There had been a time when one glass of wine was enough.

The smell of the conditioner matched the smell of the shampoo. Caro imagined that it was a rich shade of orange like the only mango she had ever eaten straight from the tree.

If they suggested she should buy the shampoo and conditioner, she would. If they asked, are you right for products, she would say, no, I need new shampoo.

Nadine had finished rubbing Caro's scalp and the water was back on. Caro did not even try to open her eyes.

'Right,' Nadine said. The water was off and she was wrapping a towel round Caro's head, pushing at her lightly to help her sit up.

Caro opened her eyes at last, and blinked as Nadine squeezed at her head with the towel then rubbed gently along the length of her hair. She wished Nadine would rub harder again, but she had read somewhere – in one of Sophie's magazines probably – that you weren't supposed to rub hard at your hair when you were drying it, because it would tangle the hair and make the ends break.

'There you go,' Nadine said. She threw the wet towels into a basket at the side of the sink. All of the towels were black. Black made them look more worn than they really were, Caro thought.

'Thank you,' she said.

'You're welcome,' Nadine said. 'Come back to your chair.'

She turned, and Caro followed her back to the chair and the mirror. Caro sat and when she looked up ready to smile and say thank you one more time, Nadine was gone.

'Right,' Suzie Woolf said. She wheeled a black trolley to the chair, picked up scissors and a comb. 'Let's get down to business.' She started to comb.

In the mirror, Caro could see Nadine carrying the basket of towels in through the swinging doors, then back out with a stack of folded towels. She thought of saying, Nadine's very good at her job, but what if she wasn't? What if she always used the wrong conditioner and bleached unbleachable hair.

'The girls should do well at netball this year,' Suzie Woolf said. 'Emma's a bit disappointed they didn't win the grand final last year. But I don't think it hurts to lose every now and then. Makes you push yourself harder, don't you think?'

Caro nodded appropriately.

'You know, the girls are lucky having Heidi Oswald for a coach. You can say what you like about that girl, but she's got a good netball brain. She's got her mother's talent there. I like to tell people how I pipped her mother at the post for best and fairest. Mind you, that was the year she left. She missed the last three games, and I still only beat her by a point.'

Caro said nothing.

'That was the bit I never understood. Missing the last three games.'

If she spoke, would Suzie Woolf stop?

'She was a tiny bit older than me, Heidi's mum, but we were quite good friends there for a while. We were out of that best-friends stage, of course. But we used to see each other sometimes in the afternoons. Chat over a cup of tea and a biscuit. She did my nails and I did her hair.' Suzie shook her head. 'We were gonna start a business together. She got a bit of money when her parents died. She was an only child, and her father had done okay out of the betting shop. We said she had the money and I had the brains.' She sniffed. 'Like either of us had very much of either. Anyway, next I know she'd been down the bank and paid off that house of hers. Said to me, "The business would have been for me, but the house is for Heidi, she can have it when she's eighteen". I just didn't understand that at the time, and I didn't . . . well, I was a bit more selfish in those days, I suppose. I was disappointed, you know.' She cleared her throat. 'We didn't see much of each other after that.'

Suzie put the scissors on their side, scraped the edge down Caro's hair. It pulled.

'Anyway, wasn't long after that, everyone's saying she's gone. They reckoned she just up and left without a word.'

She moved the stool, started scraping at the other side.

'It's funny, you know. Because she was always the first one up dancing.'

Caro watched Suzie Woolf in the mirror.

'Had a rough trot of it, Heidi has, hasn't she?' Suzie didn't pause for an answer. 'But things are starting to go right for her, wouldn't you say? I mean you'd know the best of anyone that Joel is a very good match.'

Caro winced and jerked her head.

'Sorry, love, didn't mean to pull so hard.'

'That's okay,' Caro said. She clenched her teeth against the sound of the razor scraping against her hair.

Suzie moved to the back, pushed Caro's head gently down. 'All this fuss she's started to make about the smelters and the lead.' Her voice was low again now. 'None of my business, of course, and I don't know how much you've got to do with that.' The scraping sound went on. 'It's nothing we haven't heard before. It's nothing we don't already know.'

The back of Caro's neck was tense again.

'Maybe it is a pity she never got to university. She lifted Caro's head back up then caught her eye in the mirror. 'But it's like I tell Emma, there's always more than one way to fulfil your potential.'

She put the razor on the tray, then ran a hand down each side of Caro's head. 'You do learn a lot of things being a hair-dresser,' she said, taking her hands back to the top, running them down again. 'It's a bit like being a doctor sometimes I imagine. You know, people tell you things, and they rely on you to help them make things better. And you do the best you can do at the time.'

She started the hair dryer then. The hairbrush scratched at Caro's head and the hot air blew in her ears. But there was something about it Caro liked. She was sorry when Suzie turned the hairdryer off.

'Of course we don't have laws and oaths and that kind of carry-on. There's plenty of times people do repeat the things they hear in here. All the same, there's plenty you learn that you don't tell to just anyone. Discretion.' She ran her hands down Caro's hair again, gave a small frown. 'Can't have you walking out of here lopsided.' She put her scissors down, moved around Caro, taking a careful look at her hair. Then she looked up. 'I think that's pretty right. Just a moment, I'll get a mirror, let you see the sides and the back.'

She held the mirror to the right side, the left, the back, patting Caro's hair all the while, giving small and satisfied nods.

'Don't you think . . . well, like I said, we've just lifted some of the weight. Don't you think?'

CHAPTER THIRTEEN

First game of the season today. It was in her mind before she was even fully awake. Everyone was already saying they could win the grand final this year. With Kylie back, Juliette could go into goals. The team would be great and they would win nearly every game. It was in the paper on Friday in the season preview.

Heidi had read it and thought, I could be captain of the premiership team. The article even said she was favourite for the best and fairest again. How would it be to win twice in a row! It had only happened once before. That was when Mum did it. She won two years in a row, then got runner-up, then won it again the year after that. It was on the boards in the netball rooms. Heidi looked at it every week.

They wrote that in the paper too. About Mum. Even explained about the name: 'Won it one more time, this time with her married name Oswald.'

Heidi had thought about hiding the paper from Dad, but there was no point. He'd be like a bear with a sore head if he couldn't find the paper, so she left it on the table like she always did, and he read it first up when he got home from work. Like he always did.

'Hey! Look, love! It's about you,' he said when he saw,

and she left the room as he started to read, and when she came back, he'd finished, but he hadn't said a word.

That didn't matter, though, because this could be her year. Captain of the winning team, best and fairest two years in a row, plus those kids she was coaching had a good chance too, and didn't everyone say that good things come in threes.

She was properly awake now, and there was another memory niggling at her mind. Oh. Last night. Joel.

We should start trying for a baby now.

If I wanted a baby, then maybe, she thought.

She opened the drawer of the bedside table and took out her pen and notebook. She wrote it down. If I wanted a baby, then maybe. She would keep it for a poem. She held the book open for a moment, thought about writing something more, but she started drawing straw daisies instead. One after another until they filled the top corner. She closed the book, put the pen and the book back in the drawer. Lots of thoughts and lots of words, but none of them got written down.

Heidi fell back into her pillow, tried to think the season through like Mum had taught her to do. Think of every pass you'll make, every ball you'll catch, every game you'll win.

Heidi got out of bed, went to the dressing table. She rubbed her hand across the top, because even after all these months she still liked the feeling of something new. She hadn't even guessed that Dad was doing them for her. The dressing table, the wardrobe and the double bedheads.

She rubbed at the knot on the small top shelf. He had never restored anything just for her before.

He could have made a bit of money out of this one too, because it was so beautiful and in such good nick. A full-length mirror, small drawers and shelves down each side, the large drawer at the bottom. There was a flowery vine carved across the top of the mirror, down the sides of the wardrobe, along each edge of the bedhead.

Dad hadn't had to do much in the way of repairs. Even the handles were the original ones and only one of them slightly loose.

But someone had painted it black. He had shown her when he brought it home, taken her out to the shed, made her take a step inside. She had never liked it in there. The smell was okay, but it was the dust that got into your skin and your hair and even if you didn't touch anything, the grit stayed with you for the rest of the day. Stripping this one down left black dust everywhere.

Can you believe it? he had said. What some people will do.

She had loved it even then, but she hadn't guessed he was stripping it back and polishing it all for her.

Heidi rubbed her thumb on the edge where Zac must have left a greasy fingerprint. She loved the deep colour. Not quite red and not quite brown. And she loved the finished gloss.

When Dad said he was going to bring the bedroom suite inside and give it to her for her birthday, when he said, Let's give the old one away, she had taken everything out of the dressing-table drawers and everything off the rails in the wardrobe and she had sorted the whole lot out.

Pots of cream with only smells left, knickers with too many

holes, jumpers she never wore. She had thrown two bags out and taken three down to Goodwill. It's all good stuff, it's just things that don't fit anymore, Heidi said to Elsie Levrington.

Elsie had nodded and when she opened the bags and held the clothes up to her nose, Heidi was glad she had washed them first.

In the mornings now, when she woke, Heidi knew, immediately, that everything had its place. The feeling had lasted for weeks. It made her think of doing new curtains, of getting a new cover for the bed. Out with the old, she had thought, and when she counted back, she realised the curtains had been there since she was twelve.

It was Auntie Barb who put them up when she gave new ones to Justine. Not that there's anything wrong with these: if she'd said it once, she'd said it a hundred times. If I had the money, I'd give you new ones too, but a change is as good as a holiday. Don't you think? Heidi had thought of Dad saying never look a gift-horse in the mouth, but she had never liked that shade of blue. Not because it was light, but because it had no depth.

Heidi looked in the mirror. She wasn't sure about the new curtains now. She might not be living here for long. She shook her head at herself, then looked away. Now she opened the top drawer as softly as she could. She took the nail scissors, nail file, polish remover and the bag of cotton wool. She walked back to the bed, put everything on it, propped her pillows so she could lean back into them, and got back in.

If only life wasn't happening quite this fast. Zac being sick. Dad getting Joel to move in. Too much, too fast.

She took the nail polish off first, the new red polish she'd bought to wear this week. She always bought a new one the week before the season began. Once netball season started there were no coloured nails for a while because you couldn't wear colours on short nails. Once your nails were short, the polish had to be clear. Colour looks shit on short nails, and your fingers look too stubby. Some girls did it, but it looked like shit. You should only wear clear on short.

She slipped her thumb and a finger through the handle of the scissors, held her other hand in front of herself, took one last look at her nails. The nail polish remover had left her nails with milky streaks, but they were all still long and beautifully shaped. Not one of them had broken for about three weeks. She cut her thumbnail first. That was the one that she liked the best. That one and her little finger nail. They both grew in nice shapes even without being filed.

Her thumbnail was strong and stayed in one piece, even as she cut her way around. She pulled at the last bit so the nail would not get lost in her bed. She turned her hand over, put the nail in the palm of her hand, looked at it a while, then put it in the envelope. It made a scratching sound on the paper.

It was Mum who had made the first envelope. The year she gave Heidi nail polish for Christmas. Not quite orange, not quite pink. Like the sauce the pub put on the prawn cocktails.

Every Sunday night, Heidi held out her hands while Mum brushed the polish on. When she'd finished, Mum put the manicure basket on the floor, then read stories while Heidi lay with her hands in the air until the nail polish dried. She hadn't known the trick about holding your hands in the freezer then. She did that every Sunday night until the netball season began. Then, on the Sunday before the season started, Mum cut their nails short, filed them, and put clear polish on. Heidi watched Mum drop each nail into an envelope and say, Twenty nails in all. And later on, Heidi saw Mum pull a box out from under the bed and put the envelope in.

Heidi hadn't thought about the box straightaway when Mum left, and by the time she thought to look, the box was gone. She wanted to know whether Mum took it, or Dad had thrown it out, but it was just another question she couldn't ask.

Heidi rested her hand on her knee as she filed, lifting it every now and then to check the shape. Her hands just didn't look the same with short nails. She held her hand up one last time, then stretched out her arm. They let you leave your wedding ring on, if you taped it up. Wedding ring, but not engagement.

There were people who held your jewellery for you. The ladies who scored. The ones who came to watch. But it wasn't safe. Not as safe as leaving it at home.

She took off the ring, put it on the table next to the bed, closed her eyes, and tried to think the season through. Think of every pass you'll make, every ball you'll catch, every game you'll win.

CHAPTER FOURTEEN

She heard his car in the driveway at ten, although he had said he would be there at eleven. She had only just finished mixing the cake and did not have her lipstick on. She met him in the driveway. He had a suitcase in his hand.

'Is that all you've got?' she asked.

'I always travel light,' Joel said

What does he mean by travel?

Standing on her toes, she kissed him once on the cheek, then softly on the lips and they walked inside holding hands. She liked the way he laced his fingers with hers as they walked. Dog walked behind.

'Wait here, Dog, I bought you a beautiful bone yesterday,' Heidi said when they got to the back door.

Dad was still reading the newspaper at the kitchen table, with Midnight on his lap. He stood up when they came inside, holding Midnight in one arm.

'Howdy, Joel.' Dad held out his hand. Joel let go of Heidi's hand, took Dad's and shook it.

'Peter,' he said and nodded his head just once.

Heidi liked the look Joel gave to Dad, but she did not like them shaking hands.

'You can take your bag to the room,' she said. She did not know whether to say my or our. 'I'll put everything away later on.'

She took the bone to Dog, threw it in the yard. She did not stay to watch, but she heard him yelp and bark, then growl.

'It's all right, girl,' Dad said. Midnight sat up on Dad's lap, rubbed her face into his. 'Beautiful girl,' he said.

When Joel came back into the kitchen, Heidi said, 'I'll be Polly, shall I?' Which was one of Mum's stupid sayings. 'It's time for a cup of tea,' she said in case Joel hadn't understood.

'All right if I sit here?' Joel said. Dad nodded. Joel pulled out the chair and it scraped loud against the floor.

Heidi carried the pot, the cups, the milk and the sugar to the table. 'There's biscuits,' she said, 'but I haven't finished the cake.'

'That's beaut, love,' Dad said. 'Can you get me a pen?' He turned the pages of the paper, folded it in half.

'Yeah, thanks,' Joel said. He looked at her and smiled. It was the soft smile. The one that felt like it only belonged to her.

She took a pen to Dad then went back to the bench and finished scraping the cake into the tin.

'What's a four-letter word for neat?' Dad said. 'Ending in Y.'

'Tidy?' Joel said.

'Could be.' Dad sniffed. Don't turn around, Heidi told herself. 'It's the simple ones get me every time.'

'Four-letter word for oppose. Ending in Y again.'

'Don't know,' Joel said.

'I reckon it's defy,' Dad said. 'Yeah, that fits. D.E.F.Y. See what I mean? Sometimes the harder they are, the easier they are to get. That's the way my brain works anyway.'

Heidi opened the oven door ready to put the cake on the top shelf. Shit. She had forgotten to heat it first. That would add another ten minutes, at least. She looked at the clock. They would have to eat it after lunch. Afternoon tea. They would have a proper afternoon tea.

With a tablecloth? No. She shook her head to her self. No tablecloth.

She put the cake on top of the stove. It was no good having it in while you waited for the oven to heat, you would never know where you were then. Cakes need to be done by the book, Auntie Barb always said. And that's another thing your mother never understood. Auntie Barb was an excellent cook, and she did everything by the book.

Heidi gave Zac the mixing spoon and Joel said, 'Can I have the bowl?'

Heidi looked at him and smiled. Even if it was a joke, she took it to him with a teaspoon to scrape it out.

'Want to sit on my lap, Zac?' he said. 'You can help me if you like.'

'Don't spoil the boy,' Dad said. 'He's already had the spoon.'

Zac went to Joel.

Joel made aeroplane spoons, and he said zoomzoom, zoomzoom. Heidi wanted to say, He's way too old for aeroplane spoons, but Zac was laughing.

'More?' said Joel. 'Are you sure?'

Zac laughed some more.

'How about if I take Zac to the playground for a while?' Dad said. 'Keep him out of your hair while you get unpacked.'

'Are you sure?' Heidi asked. Dad had never taken him to the playground before.

'Course I'm sure,' Dad said.

'Can we take the footy?'

When did he get old enough for footy? Heidi thought. Not that he could mark it or kick straight.

'You need your shoes,' Heidi said. 'And don't go on the rubber swing. The screw's loose and the chain keeps coming undone. And if he goes on the roundabout, you need to keep it slow.' She was talking to Dad now. 'He says faster faster, but if you go too fast, it isn't safe.'

'He'll be right with me,' Dad said. 'I am his grandpa after all.'

'You can take Dog if you like,' Joel said. 'I've got his lead in the car.'

'Yeah. Let's take Dog,' Zac said.

'Not this time,' Dad said. 'It's just you and me for now.'

The house was quiet when they'd gone. Heidi put the cake in the oven.

'We'll have lunch when they get back,' she said. 'Is that okay?'

Joel nodded, then he grabbed her hand and pulled her into the bedroom and kissed her hard on the lips. She wanted to do it, she really did, but there were all his clothes to put away, and she felt too strange, worried that Dad would come home and they wouldn't hear. And what if Zac saw? She pulled away.

'Let's just . . . I dunno . . . get everything sorted out first,' she said.

Joel sat on the very edge of the bed and looked at her, but he did not smile. His arms were crossed against his chest.

'Don't be cross,' she said.

'I never get cross with you,' he said. He smiled, but his arms were still folded.

'Can you lift the bag onto the bed?' she asked. 'It'll be easier that way.'

They had a different smell to her clothes. A different washing powder. She liked the smell, but she wouldn't ask Libby which washing powder she used.

Heidi had cleared two drawers, a shelf and some hanging space during the week. It wasn't hard, there was still room from when Dad first brought the furniture in. But it was only this morning she had remembered the letters, her diary and the photographs, and pushed them into a box and put the box on the top of Zac's wardrobe.

'Where's Dog gonna go?' Joel said. 'I could put his blanket down there at the end of the bed.'

'He can't sleep in here.' Her hands were on her hips. 'He's a dog.'

'Yeah, but he's an inside dog. Dog always sleeps inside,' Joel said. 'In my room.'

She had known, of course she had known, but she hadn't thought Dog would do it here.

'We could get him a kennel,' Heidi said. 'Dad's probably got something in the shed we could use for now.'

'He's not an outside dog,' Joel said. 'He's always lived inside.' He looked at her. His mouth was smiling, but his eyes were not.

She thought of taking his hand and rubbing it against her cheek, but he had pulled a packet of cigarettes from his pocket.

Don't do that, she wanted to say, you shouldn't smoke in my room. But she had always let him before.

She moved closer to him, kissed his cheek, then rubbed her cheek against his.

'I don't think . . . I think Dad . . .' she said, and she looked around, looked back to Joel, dropped her voice. 'Midnight sleeps inside. You can't have a dog and a cat. Not two of them living inside.'

She stood up as Joel lit the cigarette. She turned her back and started to put more clothes away. She heard him blow out smoke with a long, strong breath.

'It'll be different when we've got our own place,' she said. 'It's just, you know . . . it won't work here.' She turned to look at him again and smiled. 'Dogs take up a lot of room.'

Joel shrugged. 'I need an ashtray,' he said, and looked around like he was expecting one to be here.

'I'll get you one,' she said.

She went to the kitchen, got the green ashtray out of the cupboard under the sink. She took it back to the bedroom, put it on the dressing table so that he would at least stop smoking on the bed.

'Thanks,' he said, then stood, walked over to the ashtray, picked it up, walked back to the bed and held it in his hand, flicking his cigarette. He watched the smoke, and not her.

'Is anything wrong?' she asked softly. 'Are you okay?'

'Maybe we should wait. Or find our own place. We don't have to buy. We could rent for a while. No one can afford to buy a place straightaway.'

'We'll work something out about Dog,' she said. 'Just give it a bit of time.'

'Are you sure . . .' He looked at her, then started again. 'Does your Dad really want me here?'

'Of course he does. It was his idea.'

She looked at him, and she wondered again, How on earth was this going to work. Balancing Dad, Joel, Zac and Dog. How was she going to do it?

'We should get married right now. Find a place of our own,' he said, then took a drag on his cigarette, held his breath for a moment, pushed the smoke back out. 'We should get married as soon as we can.'

Heidi felt her shoulders drop and her head fall a little to the side. She walked to him, took his cigarette and stubbed it out, then put the ashtray on the floor. She put her arms around his neck and kissed him on his lips. They were dry, but soft and cool.

CHAPTER FIFTEEN

So I thought, Why don't we have a ladies' night, Libby had said on the phone. An early baby shower, I thought. And I was going to ask everyone from netball, and some of the school mums Heidi sometimes talks about. And then I thought, No, this is good chance for just the four of us to catch up. The girls of the family.

And wouldn't I like to be a fly on that particular wall, Vicki had said when Caro told her about it at work the next day.

No, no, she really means it, Caro said. She really wants us all to be friends.

Well, if that's what you want to believe, you go right ahead. I can't wait to hear how it goes. Vicki had laughed, then blown on her coffee before she looked at Caro and asked, Did you have that word with Heidi yet? About Zac and me? Caro had to shake her head.

It's just . . . well, you know how things are.

Caro did know how it was for Vicki, trying to fit everything in. Attaching significance to everything you did. This place, this meal, this person. Until you got to a day where you knew you never could get everything done. Where you knew that time was finite and all that really mattered was what you already had. But it was no use telling Vicki that, because when you tell people, they hear you, they nod and they think they understand. But until they get there, they never really know.

I will, I'll do it, Caro had said, but she stopped short of saying I promise.

Well, I can't come, Sophie had said when Caro told her about Libby's idea. I'm staying at Emma's. You already said I can.

You'll have to tell her you can't come. Not on Friday night anyway.

I can't. Sophie sighed dramatically.

Heidi will be there. I thought you said she's great. You can go to Emma's next weekend. I'll even drop you off myself.

Mrs Woolf's going to french plait our hair, Sophie had kept arguing. She's going to teach me how to do it.

I said you can go next weekend, Caro said. But this Friday night, we're going to Gran's.

Caro didn't know how, but she had beaten Sophie, and on Friday night Sophie was sitting next to Caro in the front seat of the car, the platter balanced on her lap.

Bloody platter. Caro had been planning it all week. Devils on horseback, mushroom tartlets and spring rolls with dipping sauce. That's what she'd planned, but the week had spun out of control and there was no Chinese cabbage at the grocer, she didn't have any unsalted butter in the fridge, and the bacon had been in the fridge at least one day too long. So it was back to toothpicks with cubes of cheese and pickled onions and a stick of kabana she picked up on the way home. The packet of

Jatz she found in the back of the cupboard was nearly empty and hadn't been properly closed.

'Don't eat anymore,' Caro said. 'There won't be any left by the time we get there.'

'How come you only ever buy kabana when we go out?' Sophie spat stale biscuit as she spoke. 'I love kabana.'

'If there's something you want me to buy, you should say.'

'You'd just say no,' Sophie said.

'No I wouldn't.'

'Yes, you would.'

'What about the jeans you asked for last week? I bought you those. And that album? I gave you money for that.'

'What about getting my ears pierced?'

'I was thirty before I got pierced ears,' Caro said.

Sophie sighed.

'Don't wish for everything at once.'

'Punch?' Libby asked when they walked in the door. 'I've made two lots. One without wine, and one with quite a bit.' She smiled at them, and Caro was glad she had made Sophie come. 'And brandy.'

'Hi, Heids,' Sophie said. She put the platter on the coffee table, sat next to Heidi on the lounge, kicked her legs out in front and crossed her arms over her chest.

Libby had Elvis on. I love my rock and roll, Libby always said. I love a good old-fashioned dance. Tonight, the sound of the music, its simple rhythm and its easy melody reminded Caro of the time when Sophie was young and she and Sean sent her up here for holidays, and when Sophie came home again she was singing 'Rock Around the Clock'. She and Sean had done the dance around and around the lounge. They sang together at the tops of their voices and it felt like the whole house shook. And Caro could hear herself, because of course she had finally said, Don't you think that's enough for now?

She accepted a glass of punch from Libby, then took a mouthful when she should have taken a sip. Why didn't Libby ever buy anything except the cheapest and sweetest wine? She'd have a hangover tomorrow even without getting drunk.

'I'll get you some more biscuits for that,' Libby said, pointing at the platter. 'I'm sure I've got another box.' She left the room, reappeared with another box, full and sealed, put it on the table without opening it.

'Thanks Gran,' Sophie said. She picked up the box and opened it, then used her teeth on the plastic wrap inside. Caro stopped herself saying, Don't do that, you'll break your teeth.

Sophie held the box out to Heidi. 'Want some?'

Heidi took two biscuits and nibbled on them.

'Cheese?' Sophie said. Heidi shook her head and Sophie took three cubes for herself.

'Would you like some cheese, Libby?' Caro asked.

'No thanks, dear, not right now.'

Caro went to the coffee table. She took three biscuits, two pieces of kabana and a piece of cheese for herself.

She looked again at the photos and trophies and souvenirs lined up on the mantelpiece. 'Thirty years service,' she said, reading the inscription on Tom's medal and shaking her head in the way Libby would expect her to.

'Yes, I know,' Libby said. 'And we were married for twenty-nine.'

'How long has your father worked there?' Caro asked Heidi.

'He's coming up for forty years,' she said, and looked down at her hands.

'Even Joel's coming up for ten,' Libby said. 'They'd have fifty years between them, Joel and Tom.'

'Joel's got a way to go yet,' Heidi said.

'He's already at seven,' Libby said. 'He's got pro-rata long service leave. The years fly,' she said. 'It'll be ten years before you know it.'

Caro leaned in even closer. *Tom Riley. Thirty years.* She put the rest of the cheese and biscuit in her mouth, then lifted the medal – it was a trophy really – from the mantelpiece. Her arm fell before she had time to adjust to the weight.

'They make them out of lead,' Heidi said. 'You look. There's a layer of lead, a layer of zinc, a layer of copper.'

'And I've heard there's gold leaf if you get to fifty years,' Libby said.

'Gold!' Sophie said. 'Do the smelters make gold?'

'Not really,' Libby said. 'There's just a bit in the ore . . . I think that's right. Something like that.'

Caro put the trophy back on the mantelpiece. She took another biscuit and a piece of cheese and sat back down.

'I meant to tell you, Heidi,' Libby said. 'I had a very strange conversation with Vicki Robbins. In the toilets the other night at the footy club.'

Caro took a drink so she wouldn't have to look at anyone.

'I mean, obviously I'm on your side . . . especially now . . . I mean insofar as there are sides . . . but even before . . . well, of course it wasn't right . . . but I think . . .'

Why is she doing this? Caro wondered. Does she think having me here makes it easier?

'It's just, Vicki Robbins asked me to say to you . . . I think . . . well, anyway.' Libby cleared her throat. 'I just promised . . . I said I'd talk with you . . . I said I'd make sure you know how things are . . . with Robbo.'

Oh God, Caro thought.

'So you do know?' Libby asked. 'About Robbo?'

'Yes,' Heidi said. 'I do. Thanks.'

'It's just . . .' Shut up, Caro thought, but Libby went on. 'I know it's none of my business, but it's just if I was Vicki Robbins . . . if it was me, I'd be asking you too.'

The silence could be nothing but difficult.

'So tell us about your wedding,' Caro said. Shit. As if that was going to help.

'Oh, yes,' Libby said, her voice too high. 'Tell us. I ask Joel to tell me what's going on, but you can't talk to a man about weddings, can you? It's like getting blood from a stone. Did you finish the invitation list? You'll have to get a wriggle-on now.'

'Almost,' Heidi said. She pursed her lips. 'It's hard though, isn't it? You know, making sure it doesn't get out of hand.' She nibbled at her biscuit.

'Oh,' Libby said. 'Yes, of course. But remember . . . well, if it's money . . . I'd be happy – honoured – to help. We didn't have a daughter, after all, and these days, when it's just me, I don't need that much. I can afford to help out. And besides, we practically paid for Caro and Sean. Didn't we?' She was looking at Caro now. 'We paid for most of yours.'

Caro nodded at Libby, then when Libby looked away, Caro gave Heidi a tiny shrug.

Elvis sang 'Love Me Tender'. It was not a song Caro had ever enjoyed.

'Have you thought about the time of year you'll have the wedding?' Libby asked. 'Spring, I suppose. When the flowers are out.'

'I get hay fever,' Heidi said. 'I sneeze and my eyes go red.'

'Yes, well, the weather's probably better in autumn, anyway,' Libby said. 'It's much more predictable then.'

Heidi shrugged. 'We really don't know. Not for sure. We'll wait and see.'

'Of course. Well, you just let me know when and where and I'll be there.'

'Love Me Tender' finished and a silence filled the room.

'Excuse me,' Heidi said, 'I have to go to the loo.'

'Of course. You know where it is. Turn the light on in the hall if you like. It does get dark down there.'

They heard the toilet door close and the latch click.

'There's nothing wrong, is there?' Libby was leaning forward, her voice low. 'About the wedding? She hasn't said anything to you, has she?'

'No,' Caro said. She tried to look unconcerned.

'She doesn't seem that happy, does she? For someone who's just got engaged.'

Caro shrugged.

'I remember when I got engaged,' Libby said. 'When Tom asked me, I was over the moon. And I remember you were the same.'

Had she been over the moon? Caro didn't remember that. She remembered happy and she remembered safe, but she didn't remember over the moon.

Sophie was looking at her now, so Caro smiled.

'And I know I'm biased, of course, but you'd think . . . well, Joel is a good catch . . . and I wouldn't have thought it would be so hard to set a date. I mean once we have that we can start to plan and everything else will fall into place.' She folded her arms. 'Like I said, I wouldn't have thought it would be so hard to set a date.'

'Wonder if they're catching any fish?' Caro said.

'I hope so,' Libby said. 'Last time they went out . . . when was that . . . can you remember, Heidi?'

'Sorry?' Heidi said. She had just come back in the room.

'The last time they went out for gar, can you remember when that was?'

Heidi shook her head. 'A couple of months ago?'

'I don't think it was as long ago as that. Six weeks perhaps? Anyway,' Libby went on, 'doesn't matter exactly when. They brought back enough to pickle. We only just finished the last jar off last week. I should have thought . . . we didn't give you any, did we?'

Caro shook her head.

'Well, this time, you can be first cab off the rank. Another drink?'

'Thank you,' Caro said, although her head had already started to kick and she wanted a smoke. Soon enough she would want a smoke more than she wanted to avoid the eyebrow Libby would raise if she went out the back for a fag.

Libby brought the drinks back in and two packs of cards.

'Let's play canasta,' she said. 'Canasta's always fun.'

'I'm not sure I remember the rules,' Caro said. 'I haven't played canasta much.'

'You'll pick it up again quick as a flash,' Libby said. 'Clever girl like you. It's just runs and groups. You know four, five, six, or king, king, king. We'll remind you as we go. Twos and jokers are wild, the red threes are bonus cards and the black threes are stop cards. You play with Heidi . . . she's very good . . . and I'll play with Sophie. It'll be a bit like the old days, won't it? Do you remember when we used to play? You and me against Sean and Tom?'

'Yes,' said Sophie, and she smiled. It was a proper and beautiful smile.

Is that something I should remember? Caro asked herself.

'So how about you, Sophie dear?' Libby kept chatting while she dealt the cards. 'How are you settling in? You must be feeling right at home by now.'

Sophie shrugged. 'Yeah, its fine, I guess.'

They lifted their piles of cards from the table and tapped

them into shape. For a moment, there was only the sound of the cards as they sorted them in their hands.

'Do you think you remember now?' Heidi asked. 'Just try to sort your cards into runs. And don't forget you might be able to add them to mine.'

Caro did not like playing cards or any other games. She didn't like the way she felt when she lost, could never convince herself it was only a game. And sulking was so undignified. Auntie Jess had said it's from not having any brothers or sisters. Sisters teach you humility, she had said. Sean had tried to make her play. Bought a leather-bound backgammon box one Christmas. Came back from Africa with a finely carved soapstone chess set.

You should be good at games, he said. You've got that kind of mind.

Caro watched as the others took their turns, picked up one card, put another one down. It came to her turn, so she picked up a card. Ace of hearts. Aces were always good, and she liked the way the large heart looked in the centre the card. She put down the three of clubs.

'Well, that's a very unusual move,' Libby said. 'With such a small pile. You do remember that black threes are stop cards? Remember I told you that?'

Caro didn't say anything.

'Pick it up again,' Libby said. She looked around. 'No one minds, do they? If she picks it up again?'

Caro picked it up, but she still didn't know what stop card

meant. She put down the eight of spades. No one had said anything about the eight of spades.

'Heidi says you're very good at netball, Sophie dear,' Libby said. 'Isn't that right, Heidi?'

Heidi nodded. She looked across at Caro. Made some kind of signal with her eyes. Caro gave a small nod. She rearranged her cards. Could she use a black three in a run?

'Yes, she is,' Heidi said. 'She gets in the best and fairest nearly every week.'

'That's her father's genes,' Caro said, and laughed to show she didn't care. 'He was good at anything he tried, wasn't he? Not like me, I can't do a thing. I'm just hopeless at sport.'

'I'm sure you're not that bad,' Heidi said.

'Oh, yes, I am,' Caro said. 'I couldn't throw a ball to save myself. Can't even get the clothes in the laundry basket. It used to drive Sean insane.' She gave a sniffing laugh. 'And I'm quite lazy really. Sean always said I'd drive to bed if I could.'

Libby laughed. 'Really? Did he really say that? I haven't heard that before.'

It was the first time Caro had ever laughed at it.

'How about . . . well, are there any boys we should know about, Sophie?' Libby said.

Oh, God, Caro thought. What on earth was she thinking? She must have had too much to drink.

'Sophie got an A for her maths test the other day,' Caro said. She fanned a group of three sevens onto the table in front and smiled across at Heidi, but Heidi did not smile back.

Instead, she looked down at her cards, shifted some of them in her hand.

'It was easy,' Sophie said. 'I already did it last year.'

'Still, an A, that's very good,' Libby said. 'Your father was good at maths.' She stopped for a moment. 'I suppose your mother was too.'

'I used to like maths at school,' Heidi said. She was still moving her cards.

'Did you?' Libby said. 'Well, there's something I never knew.' She looked around. 'All these clever people.' She shook her head. 'All these clever people. And me.' She winked at Sophie. 'Still, I do play a very good hand of canasta.' She moved her cards back and forth in her hand for a few seconds more before she said, 'Look at that, Sophie dear. Another red canasta.' She put her last card down on the pile. 'Another red canasta, and I'm out.'

CHAPTER SIXTEEN

'Go further in,' Heidi said to Zac. 'Into the middle. You don't want to fall off.' She waited for him to shuffle in before she gave the roundabout a push. That was fast enough for a little boy, she thought, but she knew it wouldn't be long before he complained.

She held the rail and jumped on. The jump was heavy and her stomach pulled. She sat close to the edge and thought about holding her head back like Mum had shown her to do, closing her eyes, and letting her hair drag along the ground. But then Zac would want to copy her.

'It's too slow, Mum,' Zac said. 'Push it faster.'

She swivelled herself around and put out her feet to stop the roundabout. The grit on the ground dusted her shoes and the cuffs of her pants. She pressed her feet firmly into the ground to make the roundabout stop, her shoe became covered in grit. They didn't have this grit at the Pioneer Women's Park. They had bark chips there, and their swings were better too. But it was a twenty-minute walk, half an hour if Zac was tired. Plus, everyone took their kids there after school and really, she couldn't be fucked with any of them.

'Push me again,' Zac said. His arms were crossed, his eyebrows lowered.

'Okay,' she said, 'okay.'

She pushed the roundabout. 'Faster,' Zac said. 'Faster, faster.' She made it look like she was pushing it again, but it was already fast enough.

A car pulled up outside the gate. A red Torana, hotted up. She narrowed her eyes.

Was that Brad? Had his dad kept the car?

She watched as he got out of the car, walked through the gate, stopped next to the tree and stood the way he always had, one hand in his pocket, one arm by his side, the heel of one foot resting on the toes of the other.

Her heart was beating way too fast.

She looked away from Brad, gave Zac another push. She could feel Brad watching them.

She gave another push, harder than she had ever pushed Zac before. Zac squealed and laughed.

'Hold on tight,' she said. She made herself laugh.

'More, more,' Zac called. She pushed enough to keep the roundabout going for a while, then she turned. Brad was still watching them.

She walked towards him, but stopped when she was two steps away so that she could not reach him and he could not reach her. She pulled her shoulders back, lifted her chin, bit quickly on her lips. Biting your lips gives them instant colour, *Cosmo* said. And it was in *Gone with the Wind* too, wasn't it? Right at the beginning. When Scarlett is first meeting Ashley.

On the stairs maybe. Sometime at the barbecue. She put her hands on her hips.

'Why are you doing it?' Brad said. He was wearing a shirt in the kind of blue that made you notice his eyes.

She didn't say anything, but she couldn't look away.

If she kept her breaths shallow she would not breathe him in.

'Why are you doing it?' he asked again.

'Doing what?' she asked. They were the simplest words she could find.

'All this lead bullshit.'

'It's not bullshit,' she said. She did not let herself look away.

'Is it because you wanna get back at me?'

'What?'

'I heard what happened to him at school. Are you doing this to him, because you want to get back at me?'

Brad was looking at Zac. He rubbed at his chin with one hand, then crossed his arms.

'You have got no fucking idea,' Heidi said and that made Brad look back to her. 'If you think that, you're even more fucked in the head than I thought you were. Which is already pretty fucked.'

That's a good line, she thought. When she got home, she should write that down. And she kept the smile, because that was the look she wanted him to see.

She checked on Zac. He was climbing off the roundabout.

'Go and play on the swings, love,' she called. 'You can go on the tyre swing if you want.'

She thought he wasn't going to go. He was looking at Brad.

You couldn't help seeing the similarities. Every time you looked at Zac, you couldn't help seeing Brad. The wave in their hair, and the way they kept straight backs.

'Go on.' Heidi's voice was sharper than she had meant it to be.

Zac looked at her, and she thought he was going to say no, that he was going to stamp his feet, bang on a turn. But he walked towards the swings.

Heidi turned back to Brad.

'I don't do anything because of you,' she said. 'I don't even think about you anymore. Everything I do, I do for Zac. Ever since he was born, ever since I knew he was gonna be born . . . everything I've done has been for him.' She could hear the wobble in her voice, but she didn't know how to get rid of it. 'It's making him sick,' she said. 'That's why I'm doing it.'

Brad was watching Zac again.

'I want to see him,' he said.

Heidi thought of the curls he had when he had his hair cut short and she remembered how soft his hair had always been. When she had asked, he told her he washed it every second day and used whatever shampoo his mum bought. Those were the days when he laughed at everything she asked.

Does your mum have all the breakfast things out on the table when you wake up? Does she pack your lunch? Who checks your homework for you?

He laughed at her questions and pushed her hair away from her forehead, then kissed her light or hard and both kinds of kisses felt good and she liked the answers he gave. No. Yes. Dad.

'Properly. I want to see him for the day. Maybe even overnight,' Brad said. The scar across his nose had never faded.

'No,' she said, and shook her head to make it real.

She had never dreamed that she would say no to him, because even with Joel, even with marrying Joel, she had still thought of this day. When Brad would come to see them both, and this is what he would want. Her and Brad and their boy. Five years later. Nearly six. And that was still her dream.

'No way,' she said. 'No fucking way.' Her fingernails dug into her hands.

'Why not?' Brad asked.

'Why? Why do you want to see him after all this time?' Her words and her voice were soft.

He looked at her now. She could not stop herself thinking that his hair looked good like that, parted on the side. She bit at her lips and she wished he would go away.

'You know why,' he said.

She was thinking of the afternoons when they came to the park after school. All of them, not just her and Brad. They smoked cigarettes and sat in pairs holding hands and she was always the first one to say, We'd better get going, there's that test tomorrow. And everyone said, You don't need to study, and they scoffed when she shrugged and they said, You always get As. Brad always kissed her one last time before she left, and said, I'll see you tomorrow.

'You said you wanted nothing to do with us,' she said. 'It's not the kind of thing . . . you can't change your mind.'

Brad looked her in the eye. 'That's not true. I never said that.'

Heidi wanted to sit down. She wanted Brad to go away, and she wanted to sit down. She wanted to sit down and put her face in her hands. She wanted to say, I don't have to listen to this, I don't owe you anything.

'He came around one night. Your Dad.' There was no way to shut out Brad's voice. 'He told me never to come near you again and he said he'd kill me if I even looked at you. Mum was there. She'll tell you. She didn't know anything about it – about the baby – until then, but she was . . . she was really kind of nice about it . . . said of course I'd take responsibility for it. She even said . . .' He looked down at the ground, shuffled his foot back and forth. 'She said if you had to go to Adelaide to get anything done, she said she'd take you.' She couldn't help it, she looked away from him. 'Your old man said he was taking care of everything and we thought he meant . . . we thought you were gonna get rid of it.'

Heidi closed her eyes for a moment too long.

'Mum was wild at me when your old man left. I'd never seen her like it before. She said I'd ruined your life, and after all you'd been through and you looked like you were gonna make something of yourself.'

He stopped talking. He was biting on his bottom lip and he was looking at Zac again.

'I was scared. Of everything. I didn't want a baby. I didn't want to marry you. I mean . . . you know, I liked you, I loved you as much as anyone would when they'd just left school, but I didn't want to get married. So once your dad said that, I just stayed away. By the time we realised . . . when we knew you were gonna have it, Mum said we would have to work something out. But then, when you wouldn't let her see you at the hospital, and then you sent the present back, well, she said it was best to wait.'

'That's bullshit,' Heidi said. She had written the poem. Dad tried. Brad denied. 'That's not gonna work. Blaming it all on Dad.'

But she remembered the night. She remembered that Dad came back and he said, It always goes against the girl. It's wrong, but that's the way it is. We'll be right though, and it's their loss in the end. She remembered thinking it was something Mum would say.

'I've got rights,' Brad said, 'and so has he.'

How would things be if she had heard that tone in his voice before?

'I don't have to listen to this shit,' Heidi said. Her voice was low and she was thinking of how it felt to have Brad's hand around her hip as they walked. She remembered learning to walk in time.

'Yes,' Brad said. 'You do. I want to see him. I want to see Zac. Mum does too . . . and Dad. We don't want to take him away. Not from you. We just want him to meet Dad.'

She thought of how it felt to check Zac before she went to bed each night, and of how she always thought of Brad when she brushed the hair from Zac's face and kissed him lightly on the cheek.

'You're gonna have to tell him who I am someday. I mean look where you live.' He threw his arms out and she couldn't stop herself from looking around. The wattle trees lining the streets were in bloom and the breeze was a gentle one. She hadn't noticed before, but you could see the tops of the Flinders Ranges from here.

It's not ugly, is it? she wanted to say. Do you remember that swing? Do you remember kissing me at that gate?

'I mean everyone knows, don't they? He's gonna find out,' Brad said. He glanced at Zac. 'And one day, he's gonna ask.'

The grass looked lush, but she knew it was brittle couch. And there was the stack that was supposed to take all their problems away. Do you remember scrunching gum leaves in your hand to hide the cigarette smell? Do you remember my bag was white and yours was blue?

'It doesn't make sense,' Heidi said. 'You reckon Dad did all those things, but you've waited all this time. Five years since you've spoken to me. Nearly six.'

'I told you. Mum said . . . we thought we were doing what you wanted us to do. And then . . . things keep happening and you still don't change your mind. It was Mum who worked it out. That it wasn't your idea to keep us away.'

He put his little finger in this mouth, scraped it on his bottom teeth. When had he started biting his nails? He dropped his hand.

'I've only had one girlfriend,' he said. 'Since you.'

She rolled her eyes, but didn't say, God, this whole thing is crap.

He looked at Zac, then back to her. 'Does he call Joel "Dad"?'

Heidi shook her head. But he would, one day. Joel wanted him to.

'Do you think you'll be happy?' he asked. 'With Joel?'

'I wouldn't marry someone if didn't think I'd be happy,' she said, putting her hands on her hips. He looked at her and she thought, Could beautiful eyes be enough?

'Do you ever wonder . . . you know . . . do you ever think . . .' Brad stopped.

What could she say? I wake up from dreams of you and they stay with me through the afternoon.

'I'll think about it,' she said. 'I'll think about bringing Zac around. For a visit. One hour.'

'If I ring you in a couple of days? I've decided to stay a bit longer. At least another week.'

She nodded.

'I'm really sorry about your dad,' she said. Then she turned and did not look back until she heard Brad's car and then she turned again and watched as the hotted-up Torana drove off.

CHAPTER SEVENTEEN

When the back door banged and Heidi knew that Dad had gone, she went to the toilet. Just to check. She pulled up her skirt, pushed down her knickers, sat on the seat. Nothing there. She pushed inside, but even before she looked at her fingers, and even before she looked into the toilet bowl she knew there was nothing there.

It had been this way before, when she realised she was late and it was four days, a week, three weeks, a month. Over a month. Two. Shit. Shit and fuck. Her rags still hadn't come. She was still at school then, and she went to the toilet when she woke up, after breakfast, after her shower, when she got to school, at the end of lessons, at the beginning of lunch, halfway through lunch, at the end of lunch, after school at school, after school at home. With no sign of blood on her knickers or on the paper, she stuck her fingers up there. She stuck them up, and she wriggled them back and forth a bit until it almost hurt and they came out again without a sign of blood. Shit. Shit and fuck.

She rested her elbows on her knees, put her face in her hands.

She shouldn't be feeling this way. Her heart shouldn't

thump and her stomach shouldn't knot. Everything was different now, it wasn't like before. She had a fiancée this time. Someone who loved her and would love their baby too. We'll have heaps of beautiful kids. Isn't that what Joel had said?

Heidi stood up, pulled her knickers and skirt into place. She flushed the button, even though she hadn't done anything, hadn't even put toilet paper there.

She went back to the kitchen and sat at the table. Her head was back in her hands. She could hear Zac up in his room. She should go to him, get him dressed. School would be starting soon. She looked at the mess on the table, sighed and felt her shoulders sag. Making the effort to stand, she went to the radio and turned it on. They'd read the stars soon. She began putting food away. Cereal in the cupboard, butter in the fridge, sugar on the bench.

The money caught her eye as she moved. Buy yourself something nice . . . you deserve a treat. Dad had given her the money last night. There's the electricity to pay this week, she had said, but he said, Never you mind, I'll leave it here just in case.

She should put the money somewhere before it got lost. After she dropped Zac at school, she would go for a walk and pay the bill at the post office. Then she would go to Sugar-n-Spice and order an iced coffee with an extra scoop of gelati instead of cream.

Heidi stacked the plates in a pile, spoons and knives on top, carried them to the sink. She turned on the hot tap, flicked her fingers under the water until it had warmed up, put in the plug, squeezed a shot of detergent under the running water, dried her hands on the tea towel, put on the gloves, turned off the tap.

First the glasses, then the teacups, plates, bowls, knives, forks and spoons. All in order. Then the saucepan from last night, the one she had left to soak.

The stars had started. Virgo, Scorpio, Sagittarius. She stopped washing and listened, waiting for Capricorn. *Your indecision will have others scratching their heads, but you will find understanding from friends you have recently made.*

She pulled out the plug, swirled at the water with the dish mop, and when she turned the tap off hard, the water hammered through the pipes. She turned the tap back on and the hammering stopped. She turned it off gently, then pulled off the gloves and draped them across the tap.

Four days since she had said to Brad, I'll think about it, and he had said he would ring.

She should tell Joel. Before Brad rang. She should meet Joel after work and tell him then. It's not definite, but I'm pretty sure . . . he would pick her up and twirl her around and throw whoops into the air. And then, later on, tonight, in bed, she would lie next to him and say I hope it's a girl and let him make jokes about enough boys for a footy team. They would make a list of names and keep it by the bed. He would laugh at the choices she made and say, There's no way I'm calling my child Blair. She would make jokes about fathers who faint when they cut the cord and who never get up in the night. More years of nappies, she would say in that way that meant she didn't care.

She bit at her lips then rubbed at her head so hard that it almost hurt.

Fuck.

One hand went to her stomach and she rubbed it gently up and down.

Fuck.

Heidi went back to the table, leaned across, picked up the money, pushed it into her pocket. She would go and look in More than Jeans.

CHAPTER EIGHTEEN

'What's wrong?' Caro asked. Vicki Robbins' face looked terrible all screwed up like that.

'I can't stand tea without sugar or milk,' Vicki said, looking into her cup of tea.

Caro pushed the sugar bowl along the bench.

'There's fifteen calories in a teaspoon of sugar,' Vicki said. She took another sip and pulled another face.

'Fifteen calories won't kill you,' Caro said.

'Every little bit hurts.' Vicki patted her hip with her spare hand. 'I'm gonna get rid of this if it kills me.'

'Oh,' Caro said. It was hard to know what to say when people told you they were on a diet.

'It's all right for people like you. Don't know what over-weight is.'

'You're not overweight,' Caro said. It sounded like the right kind of thing of to say.

Vicki held up her hand, wriggled her fingers. 'I don't like it when fingers get too fat for their wedding rings.'

Caro had never thought about it before, but with Vicki's fingers wriggling like that she could see. Fat fingers with rings did say something about a person.

'You've got Heidi coming in this morning,' Vicki said.

Caro held up her hand palm out and turned her head.

'I know,' Vicki said. 'I know . . . and I'm not . . . I'm not trying to find out why . . . it's just . . . she told Brad we could see Zac . . . and then a few days later she rang him and said the whole deal was off.'

Caro said nothing.

'And, well . . . you know he's always held a bit of a candle for her, and I think he thought she was reaching out . . . but now it's bang! Shutters down again. So I was just hoping . . . if you get a chance . . . can you just let her know . . . I don't know . . . just let her know how disappointed we are.'

Still Caro said nothing, let nothing show on her face.

'Right, well, I'd better get to work,' Vicki said. 'Another day, another dollar.'

You're supposed to say that at the end of the day, Caro thought. She took her coffee to her room.

'Well,' Caro said when Heidi was there, across the desk. She looked down at the notes and picked up a pen. She wasn't surprised at the latest results, not completely surprised. She probably hadn't expected the levels to go up like they had, but she hadn't thought there would be much change. 'Zac's levels have gone up just slightly,' she said. 'Not a lot, but they have gone up.'

Vicki had tidied the bloody desk again. Caro ran her fingers through her hair. Her desk didn't work in a tidy line of piles. Even colour-coded piles. And Vicki had wiped the coaster free of coffee rings. Caro liked coffee rings. Coffee rings and red wine stains. They made you look more interesting than you really were.

'Right,' Heidi said. 'And what about the other tests? The developmental ones.'

Caro rattled through her notes, although she already knew what they said.

'His speech and his coordination and so on – they do show that there are some very slight delays in his development. But I'd like to stress that they are generally in the normal range and even at their worst, all they're showing is a very slight delay.'

'What does that mean? Delay? What does that mean?'

'There are some things that we would expect a child of his age to be slightly better at.'

'Right.' Heidi rubbed at her eyes and then her nose and then her chin. 'So what are we going to do about it next?'

Shit. Caro still hadn't worked out what she was going to say. She had been on the phone to the minister's office every day last week, but she hadn't changed anybody's mind. She'd tried James Sanderson who she knew from med school days, but he hadn't been much use. There's not a whole lot more I can do at this stage, he had said. Minister's not interested. Not this close to an election, not with things this tight. You know how people are with these things. They take it personally and they vote accordingly. And the company did build that stack. 'Demonstrated goodwill' the minister calls it. He won't be rocking the boat over this one.

Caro had protested: But it doesn't all come down to a

workshop and a dusty house. You should see her house . . . you could eat off that floor.

It's only one child, James Sanderson had said, And you know as well as I do there's kids living on main roads with higher lead levels than his. Kids living next to powerlines, up close to mines . . . it's an industrialised world and we're all part of it.

But if there's one child, there must be more.

You don't have to convince me, but not everybody's seeing it the same way. I can point to one piece of research, they can point to another . . . plenty around to say even the level Zac is showing won't do anyone long-term harm. The CSIRO's got some projects going on, they'll be able to release their research in a year or so. We might be able to do something more then.

And in the meantime, what do I tell my patient? Caro had asked.

Tell her to get her friends to get their kids tested too. Tell her to get the whole town on her side. Either that, or tell her people have lived in that town for over a hundred years. That's the truth of it right there.

He had finished the conversation with a bit of gossip about a mutual friend's promotion, then hung up. Which left Caro here now, still asking herself, What was she going to tell her patient? What could she tell Heidi?

'If there's lead in the house, will the rest of us get it too?' Heidi spoke quickly, more harshly than she usually did.

'High lead levels aren't good for anyone,' Caro said. 'But

they are much less serious in adults than they are in children.' She clicked at the pen, then tapped it on the desk again. 'Having said that, if you were pregnant, then I would strongly recommend that we test your blood too.'

'I am,' Heidi said. 'I'm pretty sure I'm pregnant.'

'Right.' It had only been a hunch, and Caro wasn't often right. She wasn't one of those women, those doctors, who looked at a woman and knew. But there was something about her at Libby's dinner the other night. Not just the way she poked at her food, and refused a glass of wine. But the way she'd taken her hand away from Joel's, and the words she'd snapped at him.

Caro asked the usual questions, when was your last period, are your periods regular, then said, 'Well, I think you had better have a blood test.'

She took a quick look at the clock. Already behind. She'd have to send Heidi over to the lab for the test. She reached across the table for the pad. She would write as she talked.

'Would it hurt the baby?' Heidi asked. 'The lead?'

'We can't really say for sure,' Caro said. 'I'd like to see the results of your test before I say too much.'

'Right,' Heidi said.

Caro looked at the girl, at her drawn face and her lifeless eyes.

'What we can say is that having had one successful pregnancy, your chances of another are very good.'

'My mother had three miscarriages. After she had me.' Heidi was looking down at her hands again.

Caro tapped her pen on the table.

'Did she ever say . . . did anyone ever try to identify the cause?' They might have, Caro thought. At three, someone might have started to look. Or, more likely, she had just given up. Caro wrote herself a note to look for her mother's records after Heidi had gone.

'I don't know,' Heidi said.

'I know it's hard,' Caro said, 'but you really should try not to worry. Let's just wait until we've got back these results. Confirm the pregnancy. Find out what your blood lead levels are. Once we've done all that, we'll talk some more. Okay?'

Heidi nodded.

Caro looked back down, finished writing the order for the bloods.

'You won't say anything, will you?' Heidi asked. 'It's just that Joel doesn't know,' Heidi said. 'That I might be pregnant.'

Caro thought of the day when she and Sophie had just arrived and they were all at Libby's barbecue. She remembered how it felt when Joel's hand had squeezed at her shoulder and later when she took a cigarette.

'You're my patient when you're seeing me here. I won't say a word.' She handed the form to Heidi.

'What about Vicki Robbins? Will she know?'

'I've told you . . . as soon as I realised the relationship between the two of you, I made it very clear that she was not to handle any of your records.'

'Do you trust her?' Heidi asked.

'We have a system in place,' Caro said.

Heidi reached out and took the form. Her hands were shaking.

My hands shook too, Caro remembered. All those years ago. Because how stupid had she been? Getting pregnant, that was stupid enough, but not to even know. Not to even realise until all her choices were gone. What kind of doctor would she make? Caro still felt stupid, even now. To be pregnant and not even know.

She could give names to the feelings now. She'd felt suffocated. Trapped. One night she had called it entombed. It had worked out all right, of course it had. Once you had a child, you'd never wish it away. But she had not known that at the time. Lying in bed, listening to Sean, feeling the baby kick, she could not see any happy times. Barely graduated, she was working more hours than she was not. So tired at times she could hardly walk. Wanting to win this scholarship, work with that surgeon. Always having to be twice as good as the men just to stay in the race.

Trying to wish the baby away.

'Go and get the blood test,' she said. 'Then come back tomorrow and we'll have a bit more of a talk about things. You have options. There are choices you can make.' Although possibly not many. Caro kept that thought to herself.

'Can't you do a pregnancy test here?' Heidi asked.

'Yes, I can,' Caro said. 'But I think in the circumstances, I would prefer that we get the blood test done. It's more reliable.' There were no lies in that. 'And if you go over to the lab, the results will be back quicker. Probably tomorrow morning.'

Heidi nodded.

'You forgot to say congratulations,' Heidi said. Caro looked at her, not sure what she was supposed to say.

'Congratulations,' she said.

'Thanks.'

Heidi's tone was the same as Caro's had been.

Caro took another look at the clock and she hoped that the rest of the day would be conjunctivitis, chickenpox and colds.

CHAPTER NINETEEN

The laundry floor was cold, even through her socks. She could get another pair of socks or the slip-on thongs from under her bed, but Heidi knew if she left she wouldn't come back to the ironing tonight and Dad needed his shirt for the morning, and all of Joel's things still had to be done.

The iron ticked itself warm and the collar was first. The sound of the iron and the points of the collar made Heidi think of Mum and wonder, Why did she teach me to iron, but not to sew?

The part after the collar, what's that called? She reached for the word. Is that the yoke? If she had learnt to sew, if Mum had taught her or she had been listening in home ec. classes, she would know for sure. Collar, yoke (if that's what it is), cuffs, then sleeves.

You need to set the sleeves up carefully, and it's quite a trick, flattening down the seams and not doubling up the fold. No tram lines. They were Mum's words.

She looked at the crease she had just made and it followed only part of the stripe.

'Fuck,' she said to herself.

'You okay, love?' Dad asked. His voice came from the kitchen.

'Yeah, I'm fine.'

Heidi felt the heat of the shirt on her hand, heard the creak of the board, saw the kink of the cord. All of these things made her think of Mum and of being a little girl standing in the laundry door and asking, Mum can we play now?

The iron sighed with steam as she rested it on its base. Was that asbestos, that piece of grey at the end of the ironing board?

'You'd tell me, wouldn't you? If there was anything going on?' Dad was standing at the laundry door. His voice was gentle enough.

'Yeah, of course,' she said. 'There's nothing going on. I'll put on the kettle in a minute. Go and sit down. Your cup of tea won't be long.'

Go away, she thought.

The shirt was on its hanger now, the hanger hooked over the laundry door and she began again. Collar, yoke, cuffs then sleeves.

'Just you've been a bit up and down lately,' Dad said. 'Bit more down than up? Are you sure there's nothing going on?' And because he bloody well asked, the tears came and once they'd started, tears were hard to stop.

'Oh, love,' Dad said, and he held out his arms and she let him hold her like he always had before.

Why did it feel like this? Why did it feel the same this time as it had the time before? Like she was all alone. Why did it happen like this, and why did it happen to her?

Dad patted her back and stroked her hair. 'Hey, hey, love,' he whispered. 'Don't cry, it'll be okay.'

She closed her eyes as she rested against his chest. His shirt was scratchy against her cheek. He smelt like the end of the day and she breathed it in. It was how he had always been. She thought of the days when she was four and five and six, and if he wasn't sleeping because of shifts, they would play in the late afternoons. And she thought of the days when she was ten, eleven and twelve and he read the paper while she cooked the tea. That was before the meals had seemed like work. That was when people still said, You're a good girl, helping your old man like that.

She stopped the tears, but she stayed leaning against his chest, his heart beating fast and loud.

She remembered another time. A Sunday night. The television on and she was curled in his lap pretending to be asleep, but counting the beats of his heart. One-two, one-two, one-two. Mum was talking. Heidi remembered the feel of Dad's hand rubbing up and down her arm. His heart got faster – one-two, one-two, one-two – and she heard Mum say, Let me take her, let her go. Mum had lifted Heidi out of Dad's lap and carried her to bed, tucked her in and kissed her goodnight. Through the slits of her eyes, Heidi had watched Mum walk away and that's how she knew Mum stood and looked at her before she turned out the light. I love you, my darling girl. I love you.

Was that the same night she'd followed Mum to the wharf? Or was it the night before Mum left? Was that Mum's last goodnight?

Heidi pushed away from Dad, walked through to the kitchen, went to the sideboard and took a tissue to blow her nose. The tissue lasted for only one blow, so she took another one, blew her nose again. She threw the tissues in the bin without looking at Dad.

'I must be coming down with something. I've been feeling really off all day. I hardly slept a wink last night, and I had a thumping headache when I woke up.'

She blew her nose again.

'I'll get your cup of tea on now.' She picked up the kettle, took it to the sink, filled the kettle from the tap.

'Why don't you sit down for a while?' Dad said. 'I'll make the tea and you can finish that lot off in the morning.'

Yeah, okay, let's play. They'll still be there when we get back. It was another one of Mum's sayings. The vacuuming won't go anywhere. There's plenty of time to finish the washing tomorrow. Let's do something fun instead. And that was when they went for walks or paddles at the beach or picked through the boxes of buttons at the bric-a-brac shop.

'Maybe I will. Thanks. I probably just need an early night,' Heidi said to Dad.

She pulled the plug, watched the water bubbling around the hole. She filled the saucepans with water, left them on the sink to soak. That's what Mum had always done. They'll be even harder tomorrow, Auntie Barb would say and Auntie Barb was right. But Heidi was too tired. She was too tired for washing up, she was too tired to scrub, and she was too tired to think about how hard tomorrow might be.

She stretched Glad wrap across the plate she had saved for Joel, slid it into the fridge.

'Off you go, love,' Dad said. 'You go and sit down. I won't be a moment.'

She went into the lounge room, turned the television on, sat down. She stretched her legs along the lounge. Her feet were still cold and if she'd had the energy, she would have got another pair of socks.

She let her head fall back and closed her eyes for just a moment, rubbing at her stomach and remembering when Zac was in there, and all she could think was, If only this baby had a Dad.

'Here you go, love,' Dad said.

She jumped and sat up just enough to drink a cup of tea. 'Thanks.'

'Brought you some dry biscuits too. With cheese. And vegemite.' He put another plate on the coffee table.

Slithered almonds, that's what she needed. Slices of orange, and soft dried apricots.

'I remember how you used to like them sometimes,' he said. 'When you weren't feeling too good.'

'Mmm.' She would not let him catch her eye.

You don't know, Brad had said, what happened with your dad and me. Do you?

Dad's chair creaked as he sat down.

'It's just all this wedding stuff,' Heidi said. 'And you know, the engagement and everything.'

'Right,' Dad said.

And Mum's voice was always hovering in the back of Heidi's mind, even if Mum had no real right. It's complicated, love, Mum had said. Just because people don't lie, doesn't mean they tell the truth.

'I didn't know there'd be so much to do. Invitations and food and hiring the hall. It's bigger than *Ben Hur*.' Mum's words again, not hers.

Heidi really hated the noise that Dad made in his throat when he gulped his tea. He dunked his biscuit in the cup, then slurped it down. Every man's got his flaws, Auntie Barb said. It's just a matter of taking the good with the bad.

Heidi thought again of Queensland nights and of the moment she could have decided to kiss him. I would have done it, she thought, if I'd known it was going to end like this, I would have kissed him. Some guy I hardly knew. It would have saved me in the end.

She picked a biscuit from her plate. The smell of the cheese made her stomach churn. She put the biscuit back down, took a sip of her tea.

'I think you got them mixed up,' she said. 'There's sugar in this one.' She curled her lip at Dad, although the sugared tea was good.

'I remember how you used to like that too. When you weren't feeling too good.'

Dad cleared his throat and smacked his lips together.

'I can't really hear the telly. Can you?' Heidi asked. Her voice was loud. 'It's a bit low I reckon. Mind if I turn it up?'

Before he could answer, she reached for the remote and turned up the volume one more notch than she could bear.

CHAPTER TWENTY

'It's a winter sport. In winter it rains. We don't cancel games for rain,' Vicki Robbins said. She held her clipboard against her chest.

'This is a bit more than rain,' Caro said. 'You can't let kids play in this. What's the point? There won't be any skill involved, and they'll all just go home miserable.'

'Your team can forfeit,' Vicki said. 'They don't have to play, but we don't cancel games for rain.'

'Right then, we forfeit,' Caro said. She spoke loudly and she had to stand too close to Vicki to hear what Vicki said.

'Are you the United's captain?' Vicki asked.

'No, of course I'm not their captain,' Caro said. 'You know I'm not.'

'Then you can't tell me you're forfeiting,' Vicki said. 'They all know this, you know.' She nodded her head towards Sophie's red and gold team and its mothers. 'These rules haven't changed in over . . . well, I don't know, I don't think they've ever changed. Only the captain can give official advice about the forfeiture of a game.'

'I'll get the captain then,' Caro said. She turned to go.

'She'll need to come with the coach,' Vicki said. 'In the

junior grades, we ask that the captain is accompanied by the coach.'

'Right,' Caro said. She turned back to Vicki. 'Is there anything else I need to know?'

'No,' Vicki said. 'But good luck.' She turned to another woman waiting close by.

The rain was hard and loud on the roof. It had started during the night and hardly stopped since then. There was thunder and lightning at eight this morning and the whole town had lost power for over an hour. The storm had stopped and the wind had died down since then, but the rain was pelting still. The weather forecast predicted it would be like this or worse for at least the rest of the weekend.

Caro had thought Sophie shouldn't have even come, but Sophie had insisted – What if the rain stops? I'm centre. I'll let everyone down if I'm not there. We have to go. Are you trying to ruin my life – so Caro had driven Sophie down to the courts, wanting to say, If you think you can play, then I think you can ride your bike. And at the gate Caro said, I'll come in with you, I'm sure they'll cancel and then I can drive you home.

All the one o'clock teams – all the girls and all their mothers and a swag of aunts and brothers and babies – were crowded in the clubrooms. The floor and the air were wet and the smell was moving from damp to dank.

Caro walked back now to the corner where the United team was in a huddle around Heidi, their mothers in a wider circle around the girls.

'They won't cancel, but we can forfeit,' Caro said. 'Emma just needs to tell them. And you need to go with her, Heidi. She needs to be accompanied by the coach.'

'Magpies will get the points if we forfeit,' Suzie Woolf said. 'I already told you that.'

'Well, on a day like today that isn't really relevant, is it?' Caro said, and smoothed her hands down the length of her hair. 'They can't possibly play, they'll make themselves sick.'

'We're equal second,' Suzie Woolf said. 'With Magpies.' She nodded her head to the black and white team they were supposed to play. 'We can't afford to forfeit the game to them. We're not forfeiting.'

How did the woman know these things? Caro wondered. Equal second, they'll get the points. What did it matter? It's just schoolgirl netball. She rubbed again at her hair, wishing she had bothered to keep it dry on the run from the car to here.

'I'm telling you, we're not giving the points to Magpies.' Suzie Woolf's smile was not unfriendly, but it was not the smile of someone about to give in.

'I think it's up to the coach,' Caro said. She looked at Heidi. 'Isn't it?'

'Well . . .' Heidi started, rubbing lightly at her stomach.

'It's up to the captain,' Suzie Woolf said.

'I think perhaps there's a reason that in the lower grades they ask that the coach . . .'

'The coach can advise,' Suzie Woolf butted in. 'But the captain decides. It's in the rules. I've been playing netball here since I was nine and I've been on the committee for ten years. I think I'd know. We can't forfeit.'

The other women were looking at their feet, picking at their fingernails, playing with their daughters' hair.

'What does everyone else think?' Caro said. 'I'd be interested to know.'

She looked around. They'd been on Suzie's side at first, but they were softening. She could see they were. Surely one of them would speak.

'The doctor's right,' Lucy Wright's mother said. 'They can't play in this. They'll catch their death.'

Bloody stupid words, they'll catch their death. The phrase had always annoyed Caro, but she let it go. At least the woman was on her side.

'I don't want Kylie playing,' Kylie's mother said. She looked at Suzie Woolf and then started talking again. 'I mean I know we'll lose the points, but . . . Doctor Riley is a doctor,' she said.

It was not so noisy now people from the other games were leaving. 'Why don't we take a vote?' she asked. It was a childish, ridiculous way to play, but this was a childish, ridiculous game.

'We can't vote,' Suzie Woolf said. 'It's up to the girls.'

No one else said anything.

'I'll be back in a second,' Heidi said and walked towards Vicki Robbins.

'Do you want me to come with you?' Caro called after her, but Heidi either didn't hear, or ignored her.

Caro couldn't see Heidi's face, only her gestures as she pointed to the clock and the girls and the rain. Her back was straight, her shoulders pulled back. Vicki Robbins nodded as Heidi spoke. Caro wondered what everyone else saw in the conversation between Vicki Robbins and Heidi. They probably all knew the details, more than she did. Libby certainly did. And Suzie Woolf seemed to. Caro was thinking she should go over there even if Heidi didn't want her to, when Heidi walked back to the circle and spoke. 'We can't play if we've got less than five players fifteen minutes after the game was supposed to start. If we haven't got enough by then, it's an automatic forfeit.'

'Right,' Caro said. 'Come on, Sophie, let's go.'

Sophie looked at Emma. Emma lifted her eyes. Sophie did not move.

'I'm going to talk to Kendall,' Heidi said.

Caro watched Heidi walk to the Magpies team and talk to a young woman about Heidi's age. She couldn't hear a word Heidi was saying over the rain, but she could see that Heidi was pointing in her direction. The two coaches started nodding their heads and some of the mothers did too.

'They probably won't have enough to play either,' Heidi said when she came back.

Caro looked over to the other team. That group of mothers was looking at her. Some were smiling and some were not. She nodded at them, and some picked up their bags.

'So that will be neutral points,' Suzie Woolf said. 'Two points each. And if Magpies had forfeited, we'd get the full four points.' She sighed and shook her head. 'It's not the choice I would have made. But there you go . . . I'm not the coach.'

'It doesn't hurt to not win every now and then,' Caro said.

Suzie Woolf laughed, but Caro had never been good at reading people's laughs.

'Come on, Sophie,' Caro said. 'Quick. We're going.' She stopped. 'Perhaps Emma would like to come home with us? She can stay the night if she likes. I'm sure we've got a spare toothbrush and Sophie's got plenty of clean clothes.' She didn't know why she had put in the clean.

CHAPTER TWENTY-ONE

The cemetery rested on the edge of the town where the saltbush flats began. It was as flat and as dry as any place Caro had ever seen. Its car park was ringed by pepper trees. They were right for a cemetery, but not one on the edge of a saltbush flat.

It would have been better with gums. Lemon-scented gums. They were the kinds of trees that made you think of times that might never be, and of places you might never see. Gums would be better than pepper trees.

Caro parked the car in her favourite spot. There was no one else around. She had only been here on her own once before. She hadn't known how busy cemeteries were until she had started visiting this year.

She got out of the car. The tyre tracks of the latest boys' night out were laid deep in the dirt. Caro closed the door, but she didn't bother locking the car anymore. She started her walk. She went the long way today. Through the Catholics first, past all those marble statues, Jesus and Mary and babies and angels, and the inlaid photographs. Imported from Italy, someone said. Who was it who told her that? Libby? Or was it Sean? He might have told her once when they were visiting, or one night over tea when they were still telling each other those kinds of meaningless stories.

There was a life-sized marble statue of a boy over there in the next row. She had stood and looked at it on her first or maybe her second visit to the cemetery. A car accident, she had guessed. At first she had thought it was ostentatious, but now she thought, How would it be to lose a child? If a life-sized statue helped then who was she to judge?

Today, she walked down the row where no one ever went. Where the plastic flowers had faded almost to white, where the fences were rusty and where some of the plots were starting to cave.

She looked along the row and wondered why it was that no one ever came. Not all these graves were old. Died 1962, 1977, 1983. They should still have people to visit them, shouldn't they?

Maybe when she next went to Adelaide, she should go and visit Mum and Dad. Make sure their places didn't look like this.

Aunt Dot had taken her to see them once. One Christmas Eve. They had caught the bus. The roads were busy and the driver was gruff. He drove too fast and slammed his brakes at all the lights. Caro had hit her wrist on the bar of the seat in front, and it took ten days for the bruise to go.

They went to the florist across the road. They were about to close for a week, so all they had were some roses, carnations and violets. Caro chose the violets for Mum and Aunt Dot said, If that's what you think your mother would like. The woman behind the counter had smiled. It was a nice smile, but her teeth were yellow.

Had she ever gone to see her parents again? She couldn't remember that she had. She had thought of doing it. In the week before they left Adelaide and made the drive up here, she had rung Centennial Park and gave their names.

Francis is in the Rose Garden, plot G17 and Jack is in the Memorial Wall E, row 24, the man had said. And because he had an effeminate voice and used only their Christian names, she said, They're my parents, they were both dead by the time I was twelve.

Oh, was all he had said. He waited for her to say, Thank you, goodbye, before he hung up.

Caro crunched along the cemetery path. She never brought flowers for Sean, but someone had left a sprig of dried flowers in the hole behind his plaque. It was probably Libby. Or maybe even Joel. He came from time to time. Does Sophie? Caro wondered. If she did, she never mentioned it.

It had seemed a little odd, when Libby asked. 'We were wondering, could we have Sean's ashes at Port Joseph?' Joel was standing at Libby's side.

Sean hadn't lived here for years, and when Caro had come to look, it had seemed a lonely place out here on the flat, fading edge. She didn't have a better plan, so she couldn't say no, but every now and then the thought brushed gently through her mind: Where will that leave me?

It's a gift to them, she had whispered to Sean the first time she came. Don't be mad at me, although for all she knew this was the place he would have chosen.

Sometimes, standing in the cemetery, she wished Sean

hadn't been cremated. She looked at the monuments, towering marble with statues and inlaid photographs. They were expensive and extravagant, but they were a place for a family to go. They were something to treasure, something to come and dust off.

This was nice, this garden with the plaques, but it didn't have the depth.

'Do you like my hair?' she asked Sean today. She patted it with her hand. 'Suzie Woolf did it. I went back and got her to colour it. I know, I said I wouldn't go back to her again. But there's something about her I can't help liking.'

Sean wasn't always there, but he was today. He gave her goosebumps and made her heart beat fast.

She had wondered before where he was the days he wasn't there. He hadn't gone to God, not unless both Sean and God had changed their minds. But where was he, when he wasn't here? Who was he watching and who was he listening to?

'I thought I might let Sophie buy a new pair of shoes for her work experience. It starts next week. She'll need good shoes if she's standing all day. What do you think?'

Sean didn't answer. He never did. She shouldn't be surprised. Look, I really don't mind, he would say, I think you care more than me. You do whatever you think is fair.

Long before he died, long before he got sick, Caro was tired of making every decision alone.

'It's hard trying to work out which mistakes I need to let her make,' she said. It was just a statement now, and she left the accusation out.

'The engagement party's next week. Has anyone told you that? I'm sure your mother has . . . it's all right, she's being good to Heidi. Your mother is.' She smiled to show him she was pleased. For Libby and Heidi as well.

There were ants on her leg. The small ones that seemed to be wherever you went in the town. 'I was sure Heidi wouldn't go through with it. Not that she doesn't love Joel. She does.' She brushed the ants away. Brushed so hard it was almost a slap and nearly hurt. The ants would probably die. 'She's pregnant. Heidi, I mean. You can't tell anyone, okay? No one knows except us. I don't think she's even told Joel.'

There was a silence, but it was not between them. Not like it used to be.

'Heidi's very young. Her mother disappeared. Reta Oswald. Did you know her?' She stopped for a moment. 'She would have been a bit older than you, I suppose.'

She wriggled her shoulders. The sun was warm on her back.

'She's not the first person who got married without being sure. She's not the first person who felt scared.'

She looked again at the sprig of flowers.

'Does Joel ever come and visit you?' she asked, but she didn't feel even the hint of an answer. 'Joel's gonna be thrilled when Heidi does tell him. He's been talking about having kids,' Caro said. 'You were right about that. He wants a whole brood. And he really does love her.'

She stopped for a moment.

'I'm sure she's going to tell him soon.'

Crows cawed and a magpie warbled.

'And then there's Vicki. Robbo's had some bad news. We've given Vicki extended unpaid leave. Zac.' She stopped. 'Talk about a tangled web.'

She stopped for a moment longer.

'I'm not sure of the whole story . . . why they didn't have anything to do with Zac . . . I mean, Vicki really is lovely and I'm sure she would have been able to help Heidi out . . . That bit really doesn't make sense and both of them seem to brush that part of the story away.'

She stamped her feet then leaned down to brush the ants away.

'Anyway, Heidi can take care of herself, of course she can. She's shown that plenty of times.' Caro sniffed. 'You should have seen her at netball on the weekend.'

Standing here, right here, that ring of pines so dense and close, you couldn't see the stack. She thought, I like the smell of pines better than pepper trees.

'Zac's lead levels aren't going down. They're really high. It's not good in a young child.' Caro folded her arms over her chest. 'But there's only so much I can do.' She looked around, then looked back at Sean's plaque. 'Isn't there? I mean I'm only here for a year. Only another few months, really.'

She watched the ants moving along the path. Were they running? Or was that just walking speed for ants?

'Are they natives those pines?' she asked Sean.

He didn't answer.

'I've got a bit of time today, I'm going to stay for a while.

But these ants are really annoying me. I'm just going to sit over on the bench.'

In memory of Milton Burgess. Aged 83.

'Thanks, Milton,' she said, as she sat on his bench.

She could see the stack again from here.

The sighs in the pines came and went with the breeze. Cockatoos flocked, but did not stop.

She took her diary out of her bag. Diary number seventeen. It would be full before too long. They went through patches, the diaries did. Times when she wrote every day, and a span of two whole years when she hadn't written anything at all. These days, she opened the diary a lot, but hardly ever wrote.

Caro took out a pen, opened the diary, and rubbed the blank pages with her hand. This one looked like a diary should, small and leather-bound. It was the second-best one she'd ever had. The best was the first, of course. Caro liked to think it was a final gift from her mother. Stowed away, wrapped, ready for her birthday, found in the wardrobe by Aunt Dot. Caro liked to think the gift had been deliberate, that Mum had somehow known.

Caro planned to read them all again one day. The day she turned sixty-five she would start at the beginning. It would be too late by then to worry and have regrets, but there would still be time if there were matters she had to put right.

She stood up, carried the diary and the pen, but left her bag on the bench and went back to the plaque.

'Isabelle left Graeme,' she said. 'She blames me, of course.

She's staying in the house, with the kids. He has them every second weekend.'

She looked around. There were still no other cars in the car park, no one else standing at graves.

'It's a lot to lose,' she said. It was a terrible thing to say when it was Sean who had lost the most.

'I can't say sorry again,' she said.

But she just had. There would never be a time when she did not apologise.

After he died, so many people had tried to comfort her, saying, He kept things from you so what could you do?

But how could she not notice bleeding that didn't stop and the boxes of Panadol he must have chewed his way through. He didn't want to face up to it himself. It's our subconscious, it does the strangest things.

But she'd only needed to be looking at him and she would have seen. The bleeding, his pale and thinning face, his falling energy.

She took a step to the side so that she could see the stack. She liked its grey against the afternoon blue of the sky. How did they decide how much of the top to paint black? And wasn't it strange how you never saw any smoke?

'Zac and Heidi wouldn't be the only ones, would they?'

The breeze was stronger than it had been and there was no more sun on her back. A pair of pigeons plumped their feathers at each other until one of them flew away. She should get home and start the tea. 'If I told Heidi what we had to do . . . get some of the others on side . . . she'd probably do it. She'd give it a try.'

Caro looked down at the plaque. Loving father of Sophie and husband of Caroline. It's not how she'd put it if she had to write it now.

The ants were still moving in their lines.

'I have to do it, don't I?' she said to Sean. 'I have to try and sort things out.'

CHAPTER TWENTY-TWO

She had promised herself that she would tell Joel last night. She couldn't put it off anymore, not after she'd bumped into Vicki Robbins at the supermarket, and Vicki Robbins had whispered at her, we're getting the papers drawn up. Heidi had to tell Joel, and she had to tell him soon.

She had been planning to do it all week. At breakfast every morning, she had thought, I'll tell him when he gets home tonight. And when he came home, she thought, I'll tell him as soon as we've finished tea. Then after tea she thought, I'll just get the dishes done. But every day had ended with the same thought. Tomorrow, I'll tell him tomorrow.

When he went for his shower, she stood in front of the mirror and turned herself from side to side as she stroked her stomach. And she saw that her breasts had already grown and her nipples were already dark and she couldn't be sure, but her stomach might have started to bulge. She thought, If I leave it long enough, he'll guess, Blind Freddy could see I'm up the duff.

So she had promised herself last night, she would stop putting it off.

But then, she had told him about the council meeting she'd be going to. And he had said, Why are you going? What's the point? What are you trying to prove? And it was all downhill from there.

If Zac's levels are high, then other kids' probably are too. They tested the soil in the garden and the water in the tanks. None of it's safe.

You're making up problems, I work down there, and there's nothing wrong with me.

You're not a child. She had tried to reason when she should have just shut up.

Not now I'm not. But I was. And so were you. You've lived in this house all your life and there's nothing wrong with you.

If he didn't feel it, then how could she explain it to him? She couldn't say, You don't understand, because he isn't your child.

In the end, he had turned away from her and gone to sleep and another chance to tell him about the baby was gone.

Maybe she shouldn't have spoken to the principal, she thought. Because what Joel said was true. She had lived here all her life and there was nothing wrong with her.

It was Caro who started it. When she heard about the community garden that Dad and one of the teachers had started. They should check the soil, Caro had said. So they had, but it wasn't conclusive. So then they checked the rainwater. The lead readings were high. Too high.

Follow it up. That's what Mum had said when Heidi told her about the article Caro had given her. An American town where the kids got sick. It explained the symptoms the kids were showing and the measures the smelters had to take.

It was Caro and Mum who led her into it, but they weren't here now as she walked past the 'Trespassers Prosecuted' sign and through the school playground and past the swings that Zac didn't like because he thought they might break. Someone had raked the sandpit since the kids went home, but it looked like a cat had already run through. They should cover it, Heidi thought. A tarp would do, and it would stop the cats from getting in. She should put that idea in the suggestion box.

The suggestion box. That's what she should have done. Put an anonymous suggestion in the suggestion box. Get all the children tested for lead. Then left it at that.

If she'd done it that way, anonymously, then people wouldn't have started whispering about her again. Dad would be talking to her in more than grunts and Joel wouldn't have said, with more meaning this time, Maybe I should move out. And on top of Dad and Joel and Vicki Robbins, there was always Mum. Ringing now, every second day. You've done the right thing, stick to your guns. And always, always ending, You know, if you moved up here . . .

Heidi pulled open the screen door of the classroom where they were holding the meeting, because the staffroom was being painted. That door had seemed so big when she was five. She remembered holding Mum's hand while Mum put her schoolbag on the hook over there where the books were now. These days, they hung the bags on the hooks outside, under the veranda. These days Zac held her hand.

A trestle table had been put up in the middle of the room for the night. They were all there, already sitting in green plastic chairs. She had never been into the school at night before. The fluoro lights never looked this white in the day. There were no books or toys or puzzles or anything on the floor.

Heidi was sweating and she knew that if she lifted them out in front, her hands and fingers would shake.

'Ah, Heidi.' It was Ged Armstrong. 'Why don't you sit here?' He pointed to the only empty chair, right down at the end next to him. She sat in the seat Ged offered and put her bag on the floor at her side.

She rested her hands on the trestle. Its top was cold and hard. Not what you expected a trestle to be.

She looked at Ged and gave him a little nod like she had seen people on the telly do. I'm ready. She would have spoken if she could trust her voice.

Ged looked around the table, barely moving his head as he counted one more time.

'All here,' he said.

One trestle was a bit too small with all of the committee here, Heidi thought. But there wouldn't be room for two.

Ged looked at his watch, then up at the clock. Heidi wanted to say, The big hand is on the twelve, so it's something o'clock. It was the kind of thing that Renee could say and everyone would laugh.

'Spot on time,' Ged started. 'Let's get started, shall we?' He gave a smile around the table. 'Good evening, ladies, gentle-men,' he said, 'and welcome once again. Welcome in particular to Heidi Oswald.' He turned his head a little to nod at her. 'As you know, she has come to talk to us about one of this evening's agenda items. So let's push our way through the administrative bits and pieces first, shall we, then we'll move on to the lead testing issue.' He peered at the piece of paper in front of him. 'So.' He looked around the table again. 'All present and no apologies.' He stopped and watched as Mrs Maynard took the notes. He started again when she looked up. 'Minutes of the previous meeting. Has everyone read the minutes?'

Heidi watched as everyone around the table shuffled through their papers. She kept her eyes focused straight ahead and her breaths were deep, but quiet.

'Right,' said Ged. 'That's the administration done. So let's move on to item four. Lead testing for all children at East Park Primary School.'

He stopped, looked around. 'Before we begin the discussion of this item, I would like to remind committee members that if you have something to say, you will address the meeting through the chair. I will not tolerate interruptions or interjections.' He cleared his throat, then smiled at Heidi. 'Let's begin. Now, as you will be aware . . .'

For a moment, Heidi could not hear what he said. Her heart was thumping faster than it ever had before. She wanted to close her eyes.

'So, Heidi, do you have anything to add?' Ged Armstrong asked.

She could say, No, I think that just about covers it. She could wait until someone asked her something specific.

'If you've got too much lead in your blood, it makes you

sick,' she said. It was a pathetic start. 'So we need to know whether or not it's true. Whether they have got high levels of lead in their blood. We need to know whether our kids are getting sick.'

'Thank you, Heidi,' Ged Armstrong said. He raised his eyebrows. 'Anything else?'

There was. Heidi knew there was. She had stood in front of the mirror and practised it. Practised the words she would use, the way she would hold her head, how she would move her hands. But now she was here, she couldn't remember any of it.

Mrs Maynard gave her a tiny smile.

Heidi's heart was still thumping, and she was sweating so hard it almost made her shiver. She unlaced her fingers, put her hands flat on the table.

'I have worked in that smelter all my life,' John Blake said. His voice was loud. 'And my father worked there too. And so did my grandfather.' Evelyn Stevens was nodding at every word. So was Violet Brown. And so was William Farrow. 'And I've lived down here all my life too. Are you saying there's something wrong with me?'

Evelyn shook her head.

'It's not about you and it's not about how things were back then. It's about the kids right now,' Neil Andrew said.

Irene Stone didn't say a word.

'You know if we do get this testing done, and there's nothing wrong, then that's okay. That's good. But at least we'll know,' Heidi said.

Ged Armstrong looked at her. He raised his eyebrows again. He nodded this time.

John Blake folded his arms across his chest, leaned back in his chair. 'It's a waste of money,' he said.

'She's right though,' Irene Stone said. 'If we get it done, then they have to shut up. It's a way to prove they're wrong.'

Ged Armstrong looked slowly around the table. No one spoke.

'We'll take the vote now, I think,' he said. 'All those in favour of asking that all of the children attending East Park Primary School have their blood lead levels assessed.'

Silence again.

It isn't the light that makes the room feel strange, Heidi thought. The place isn't right without the kids. No laughs, giggles, sobs. No skips, hops, runs. Classrooms shouldn't be this quiet.

Heidi watched. Neil Andrew raised his hand.

Ged looked around. 'Any others in favour?'

Heidi could feel Irene Stone next to her. She was lifting her hand from the table.

'Is that a yes, Irene?' Ged Armstrong asked. Heidi turned so she could see Irene. She was looking straight ahead and nodding her head. 'Yes,' she said.

'Against?'

John Blake lifted his arm. Everyone else followed.

'Thank you, ladies and gentlemen,' Ged said. 'With only two in favour, the motion is defeated.'

He looked at Heidi. 'The decision has been made.'

CHAPTER TWENTY-THREE

'Six hours last night.' There was triumph in Renee's voice. 'Six hours without a feed.' She held Charlotte so the baby could look around. They were sitting on a rug outside because just this week, the days had started warming up. The nights were clear and cold, but during the day the sun and the breeze were warm.

'I can't believe how good I feel,' she said. 'A bit of sleep and I feel like a million bucks! Six hours! You should see what I've done today.' She patted her hair with her spare hand. 'Shower and make-up and hair. I've made the bed, paid the bills, and I've even got a proper meal ready for tea.' She leaned back. 'How is *that*?'

'See?' Heidi said. 'I told you it gets easier. Life gets easier all the time.' Heidi smiled at Charlotte, and Charlotte smiled back.

'Oh. There's nothing like a baby's smile, is there?' she said, without moving her gaze. And that's what would make it okay. The baby's smile. Think about the baby's smile. It was days – maybe a week – since Heidi had told Joel, I'm pregnant, you're going to be a dad. He had grinned to himself and all that night he had laughed at nothing at all, but he hadn't lifted

Heidi from the ground, twirled her around, whooped or yelled. He had rubbed at her stomach, but he hadn't brought her flowers and he'd made no jokes about football teams.

'Are you smiling at Auntie Heids?' Renee turned Charlotte around, held Charlotte's face close to hers. 'Are you? Are you smiling at her?' Renee's face and voice were soft. 'Isn't she gorgeous? Yes, you are. You're gorgeous, aren't you?'

She kissed Charlotte on the cheek, then held her in one arm, rubbed at her tummy with the other hand. Charlotte chuckled.

And there's nothing like a baby's laugh. It reaches inside you, into your body and into your mind, and when a baby's laughing there's no room for anything to be wrong.

'And then she went straight back to sleep, and didn't wake up until nine. Nine o'clock!' She tickled Charlotte some more. 'I didn't even hear Tony leave.' Charlotte chuckled some more. 'I tell you, I am good at this.' Renee laughed and Heidi did too.

'I'll go and make you a cup of tea, then I'll hold Charlotte for you while you drink it hot. Make it a perfect day.'

Inside, she put on the kettle and took the box of Earl Grey out of the cupboard. She had bought it last week, on special at Foodland. She would have liked the purple box, but that was Darjeeling and it reminded her of Mum, and it would remind Dad too. So she bought the Earl Grey instead. Horrible stuff, Dad said. Tastes like dishwashing detergent. Just give me a cup of plain old tea.

Joel shrugged and said, It's okay, I don't mind, it's all the same to me.

Heidi held the box to her nose. Bergamot oil, it was. She'd looked up Earl Grey in the encyclopaedia last night and it said they mixed the tea-leaves with bergamot oil. Then she looked up bergamot. Bergamot is a fragrant citrus fruit, and the bergamot oil comes from the rind.

She waited for the kettle to boil then warmed the pot and the cups, tipping the water back and forth from each before throwing it in the sink. Two teaspoons of leaves plus one and the tea was made. She put the pot and the cup on the table then took the packet of biscuits from the cupboard, opened it with her teeth, and listened to Renee and the kids out on the lawn.

'Here you go, Teddy,' Renee was saying. 'Mmm, that's delicious.'

Zac was too old for feeding teddy bears, Heidi thought. She piled the tray with tea, cups, biscuits, a drink for Zac, and went back to the rug. As soon as she sat down, Zac climbed into her lap and she linked her hands around him. 'I was going to hold Charlotte,' she said, but she kissed the top of his head. 'I'll take her in a moment,' she told Renee.

Zac snuggled into her lap, kicked his legs one at a time. They were tiny kicks, but they pushed him against her stomach all the same.

'I went to the doctor again yesterday. The results weren't that good,' Heidi said. 'The doctor says his levels have gone up again. Just a bit, but they're definitely up.'

'Only a bit,' Zac said.

'Yes, sweetheart, that's true.' She forgot that he was old

enough to listen and take things in. 'Why don't you go and play with your Lego. Build something for Joel. You can get yourself two more biscuits on the way.'

'That's five months in a row,' Heidi said, talking to Renee after the back door had closed behind Zac. 'And even if they don't go up, they never go down.'

'Mmmm,' Renee said.

'And so are mine. My levels are up too.' Heidi remembered the edge in Caro's words. Okay, there's only so much you can do on your own, she had said. That's what I believe. There's bigger things going on. But unless we get universal testing – or even convince a good number of parents to test their kids – the government's not going to do anything. And nor is the company.

So there's nothing more I can do? Heidi had asked.

There's a television crew that could be up here by Thursday and you could tell your story to them. They'll air it early next week.

Television? Heidi hadn't understood what Caro was talking about.

Denise Maynard's willing to be interviewed and so am I. All they need to make a story is a parent. And that's where you come in.

Heidi had said no at first. No way. Fuck that. Television? They'd all hate her for sure. And, anyway, whose business was it if her kid was sick? But then she'd picked him up from school and he looked so pale . . . but still, all these people . . . they were her friends.

Charlotte smiled at Heidi.

'Has she got a tooth?' Heidi asked.

'Maybe,' Renee said. 'I'm pretty sure one's on its way.'

Heidi shook her head. 'You're not gonna be a baby for much longer, are you?' she said to Charlotte. And then she said the words she had practised in her head. 'I'm gonna leave.'

Charlotte gurgled. Heidi could hear a magpie and a car. Her leg was getting stiff.

She felt a flutter. She rubbed her stomach, but it was too early for the baby. Way too early.

Heidi wanted to speak, but she did not want to say to Renee, I have to get out of this place. She couldn't afford to say the wrong thing. Not to Renee. Not now.

'Where you gonna go?' Renee said. She looked at Heidi now.

'Queensland,' Heidi said. 'With Mum.'

'You're gonna live with her? With your mum?'

'Zac can't get better if we stay,' Heidi said. 'And I can't . . . I haven't got the money to live on my own.'

She wasn't looking at Renee now, but at the tree in the corner of the yard. At its large trunk and peeling bark. At the light in the leaves. At the swing, a tyre on a piece of grey rope, wrapped around the bottom branch.

'What about Joel?' Renee said. 'What does he say?'

Heidi leaned back on her hands. 'I haven't spoken to him yet. I've only just worked it out. Not even an hour ago.' She bit at her lip. 'You're the only one I've told. Don't say anything, will you?'

Renee shook her head. 'Course not.'

You won't tell anyone, will you? It was a chorus for their lives. That and Course not.

Course not. It's what Renee had said when Heidi told her about Zac, but Heidi still remembered the short, sharp sound of Renee's shock.

Shit! Renee had said.

Will you be its godmother? Heidi had asked.

Godmother? What would I have to do?

You look after the baby if I die. Heidi had looked away as she said the words.

Really? If you die?

Don't worry. Heidi had tried to laugh then, but it was just an ugly snort. I'm not gonna die, am I? It's just . . . you know . . . somewhere else for him to go when things go wrong.

I dunno. Renee's voice was quiet. A godmother. I'd better ask Mum. I've still got school.

'What if Joel doesn't wanna go?' Renee said.

'Zac is sick. And the baby might be too.' Heidi could smell the other tree. The lemon-scented gum that Mum had planted, snipping at the ends as it grew and saying, If it was in the bush, the kangaroos would do this. They'd nibble at the ends and it would help the trees to grow. Mum snipped at the ends of everything.

Heidi had to stretch her mind to remember how the garden was before Mum left. Before Dad pulled everything out and rearranged it all in rows. It's a much more sensible garden now, Auntie Barb had said.

'You think they're right, don't you?' Heidi said. 'You don't think I should be stirring all this up?'

'I dunno. Sometimes yes. Mostly no. I mean when you say things like "lowered IQ" it doesn't make sense. Look at you. You were gonna be dux.'

'I know,' Heidi said.

A fairy garden. There had been a fairy garden. In the corner, behind the shed. With painted toadstools and crystals and a tiny wooden door banged into the tree.

'You don't wanna have another baby on your own. That's what you've always said.'

'I know,' Heidi said. 'It's a mess. I'll be all right, I'll be with Mum.'

Renee picked at the blades of grass. 'What about . . . I mean, you always said . . . after everything she's done . . . are you sure you wanna live with her?'

Heidi looked out of the yard, past the town, right out to the hills. The light was soft enough to take your breath. There had been bells, fairy bells that tinkled in the trees.

'It's different now. Mum's worked things out. We'll be okay.'

Renee kissed her baby's head before she spoke again.

'I'll do your hair before you go.'

CHAPTER TWENTY-FOUR

'Be home by twelve,' Caro said to Sophie.

'But no one else has to be,' Sophie said. 'It's so embarrassing.'

'All right then, one,' Caro said, although she did not know why. 'But I mean it. No later than one.'

Caro liked Noah well enough. He was quick, he was funny, and when he laughed you couldn't help laughing along. But it was an eighteenth birthday party and Sophie was only fifteen. What happens to fifteen-year-old girls at the parties of eighteen-year-old boys? Caro was still deciding whether 'Sophie turns sixteen' belonged with the pros or cons about staying here next year. In five years, she told herself, I'll be ecstatic if she has found someone who treats her so well. But for now? She's only fifteen.

Want to come over Saturday night? Keep me company while I worry about Sophie? Caro had asked Vicki, because it was fun the other time Vicki came around. Loud, but fun.

I can't. It's my niece's twenty-first that night. I'm her godmother too. Her mother'll kill me if I'm not there.

So Caro opened a bottle of wine, and drank it while she watched the Saturday night movie. *Ferris Bueller's Day Off*, so it could be worse. She ate a toasted sandwich for tea. The tomatoes were sweet and it had just the right amount of cheese.

At the end of the first glass Caro thought of ringing Graeme again. But she would have to admit to him that she hadn't talked with Sophie yet. She drank another glass and she could not ring him now. He would say, Have you been drinking tonight? And he wouldn't let her say, You don't understand.

She opened a jar of olives during one of the ads, the avocado dip during another. She drank another glass of wine.

Tomorrow. She would talk with Sophie tomorrow. There's something I need to tell you, she would say. That would be a good start. But what next? What could she say that Sophie could understand? Graeme's been offered a job at the school up here. That wasn't a lie, but it would be a cover for the truth. Should Sophie know the truth or be protected from it? And if she should know, should it be all of the truth or just part of it? Once I start telling her, Caro thought, how far back should I go?

She poured herself a nightcap. A small whisky would help her sleep. It would stop her waking when Sophie came home.

The whisky did not help her sleep.

She lay in bed. Her feet were too hot. Her legs twitched. She could not even close her eyes.

It was twelve o'clock. Quarter past. Half past. Quarter to one.

She thought of having a shower, a coffee, a cigarette, another glass of wine.

One o'clock and Sophie was not home.

Quarter past. Half past. Two.

Caro thought – briefly – of what might have happened. A car accident. Too much to drink. Gone home with the wrong people at the wrong time.

The muscle in the back of Caro's neck was tensing up. She would have a headache soon. She should have had some water before she came to bed.

She got up to get a drink. Her stomach lurched. Shit. The hangover was already kicking in.

She stopped at the door of Sophie's room. It was not completely closed.

Caro pushed at the door gently. Perhaps she would see that Sophie was already there. Maybe she had somehow fallen asleep and Sophie had snuck in, missing the creaky floor-boards, not turning on the lights.

But the blind was up and the curtain had not been closed and the night's white light came through. Sophie wasn't there.

Caro walked further into the bedroom, without turning on the light. She was alert, ready to leave if she heard a car or footsteps on the drive.

She could smell that dreadful fragrance Sophie insisted on wearing. These days she sprayed it on every morning in long bursts that filled the house and made Caro's eyes water and nose run and stayed on Sophie's clothes so that when Caro sorted the washing piles, the smell hit her in sickly wafts and gave her a headache every washing day.

Caro stood at the end of the bed, looking down. She remembered the nights when Sophie was young, and Caro would give one final check before she went to bed. She thought of the peaceful look on the young Sophie's face. She remembered that she had sat on the bed and brushed Sophie's hair lightly with her hand. She had watched while Sophie slept, and she had kissed Sophie's cheek, Sophie's forehead, Sophie's hair.

She could still remember the singing in her heart.

Sophie's pyjamas – the pink ones with the small purple flower print – were in a crumpled heap at the end of the bed. There was a pile of *Dolly* magazines on the bedside table and some pulpy book folded on its spine. Caro shook her head. For a girl who was reading *Lord of the Rings* when she was ten and *Animal Farm* when she was twelve, she was reading some rubbish now.

The light of the stereo was on. Caro leaned over and turned the switch to off.

They would have argued about that stereo if Sean were alive. When Sophie had asked, Can I have a stereo? Sean would have said, Well, why don't we get her one? and Caro would have said, It's too much for a teenage girl. And in the end, Sean would have given in to Caro, and they would have given Sophie another book, and maybe some clothes.

Sophie wouldn't have that stereo if Sean were alive.

On the other side of the room, Sophie's desk and bookshelf were neat and organised. Labelled folders stood one against the other, then textbooks on the next shelf down with small pieces of ripped paper sticking from the top. Sheets of paper with long coloured lists taped to the wall. Conjugated French verbs, the periodic table of elements and quotes from *Macbeth*. The *Endeavour*, Eureka Stockade, Great Depression, White Australia.

Caro moved closer to have a look at the corkboard and its photographs. Noah with his wide grin and round eyes, his arm around Sophie's shoulders. Caro leaned even further in. It was hard to see in the dark, but there was Sophie's smile. Beaming and real. There were other photos too. Sophie and Emma. Sophie with Lucy and Kylie. Noah again. Sophie was smiling in them all.

Where was Sophie? Why didn't she come home?

Caro went to the kitchen, gulped a glass of water, filled the glass again, sat at the kitchen table. These were the times that Sean bloody well should be here.

She felt queasy and her head thumped. She picked up the packet of cigarettes and tapped it on the table before she pulled a cigarette out, lit it and took a long, deep drag.

Why wasn't Sophie home? One o'clock. Caro had said be home by one o'clock and Sophie had agreed.

Caro got out of the chair, took her keys from the bench. She would find Sophie and bring her home, but as soon as she had reversed from the drive, she knew she'd made a mistake. She should have stayed at home. She had not even pulled a jumper over her pyjamas so even if she did find Sophie, she wouldn't be able to get out of the car, she would just be able to wind the window down and yell. Not dignified.

Go home and back to bed, Caro told herself, you'll see Sophie in the morning. You can yell at her then.

The street light in front of their house was out. How long has it been like that? Caro wondered. A responsible citizen would ring the council and let them know.

The gears screeched as she changed from second to third. She pushed the clutch in and pulled herself into the steering wheel, felt the muscles tightening in her back. The nights were still so cold, and the heater hadn't warmed up yet.

On the other side of the road, a drunk on a bike teetered as he lifted his arm to give her a long, slow wave. Lucky the roads were flat and wide.

A cat ran across the road. Probably black, Caro thought.

She turned right at the roundabout and headed for the clubrooms, because that's where Sophie was supposed to be. All she'd do was check that Noah's car was there, then go home and go to sleep.

But even from the end of the road, Caro could see the clubrooms were dark. No party. No cars. No kids.

Caro turned the car, stopped at the intersection, looked from left to right. Where to go? The lights at the top of the stack were bright and one of them blinked a regular rhythm. Why did it need lights? As if any planes would be flying overhead. She looked from right to left. The houses were dark. Another cat ran across the road. The light at the top of the stack stopped blinking. Why would it stop? Caro wondered.

There weren't any cars, and she couldn't stop at the intersection all night. She had to move, but where? The beach, the wharf, the Pioneer Women's Park? Where did you go at this time of night? Caro had not been the kind of teenager who stayed out late at night. She was living with Auntie Jess by then and there was the scholarship to win.

Grab a cigarette. Push the lighter in.

She'd hardly been out at all before she met Sean and she quickly realised why when time with him had nearly cost her the third year exams. It had seemed so important at the time. She had even broken up with Sean, saying, If I fail, I lose my scholarship. He'd laughed. Come and do teaching, he had said. You'll piss that in, and there's bloody scholarships galore.

I want to be a doctor, she had said, because even if it was Auntie Jess's dream first, it was Caro's as well by then.

She took a drag. So what if I do find Sophie, and what if she is with Noah or some other boy? What do I do then? Shine the lights at the car? Bang on the bonnet, the boot or maybe the window? And all in my pyjamas?

This was stupid. She would have to go home.

But as she turned the car, her cigarette dropped on her leg. A hurried glance down, swipe with her hand, and one wheel was up on the footpath. By the time she had the car straight, it was filled with a translucent blue. A police car was in the mirror, its light flashing, but no siren sounding.

Where had that come from?

She slowed down to let it pass but it did not overtake.

Me? Do they want me? Fuck.

She pulled carefully into the curb, stubbed her cigarette, used one hand to smooth her hair and the other to wind down the window. She could not get out. Not in her pyjamas.

Two policemen walked to the car, torches in their hands.

One strode around the car while the other leaned in her window.

'Hello,' she said, because she did not know what else to say.

'Where you off to?'

'I'm looking for my daughter. I told her to be home by one, but she wasn't home, and I just thought . . . well, I thought I might come and have a look. You know what teenagers are like, she's probably home by now. It was stupid coming out like this.'

'You got any ID?' he asked.

She shook her head. 'I just left the house without thinking.'

'What's your name?'

'Caroline Riley.'

'The lady doctor?' he asked.

'Yes.'

'Right,' the policeman said, then took his head out of the window. 'It's that lady doctor,' he called.

'Oh, yeah,' the other policeman said. His torch shone through the windscreen. Caro closed her eyes against the light and turned her head away.

'My missus reckons you're lovely.' The man had his face in the window again. 'Jennifer Crosby.'

'Oh, yes,' said Caro.

'Don't know what you did for her, but . . .' his voice dropped. 'She's much *better* these days.'

'That's good,' Caro said. Jennifer Crosby. Three girls under three, husband telling her to have one more. He really wants a boy, but we were only going to have two and anyway we might never have a boy. I don't want anymore kids. I can't. Tears. Prescription for the pill. But what if he finds out, what if someone in the chemist says something? A year of repeats, so she could get it filled in Adelaide.

'You shouldn't smoke while you're driving.'

'No,' she said. 'I won't do it again. I'm giving up. Starting Monday. It's Sunday now. So this is my last day.'

'You been drinking?' he asked.

'I had a glass of wine with dinner,' she said. 'And a small nightcap before I went to bed.'

'I could take you to the station,' he said.

Caro did not respond.

'Where do you live?' he asked.

'Ethel Street,' she said. 'At the school end.'

'We'll follow you home,' he said. 'You're right. Your daughter's probably home by now. But we'll have another look around for you if she's not.'

'There's no need,' Caro said. 'I'm sure she'll be home by now. I'll be okay. And so will she.'

'Just let us follow you home,' he said. She watched in her rear-view mirror, waited for them to get in their car, put her indicator on, drove home at forty kilometres per hour, thinking, Sophie will be home when I get there, but I won't take this out on her. Tomorrow, we'll talk about it, make sure it doesn't happen next weekend. Then never talk about it again.

But when she turned into the drive, there were two other cars and the house was lit up.

She ripped off her seatbelt, opened the door, ran inside. 'Sophie? Are you home?'

Sophie was in the kitchen with Noah. And Vicki.

'God, Mum, where have you been?' Sophie's voice was so loud it screeched. 'We've been worried sick. Where have you been?'

The policemen came in behind Caro. Their shoes were loud on the floor.

Caro pushed her hair from her face. She should have put the wine bottles away, emptied the ashtray before she'd gone to bed. She should have stayed at home.

'I was out looking for you,' Caro said, keeping her voice calm. 'I said be home by one.'

'Sophie got worried when you weren't here,' Vicki said. She put her arm around Sophie. 'So she rang to see if you were with me, and I thought I'd just come round. I told her you couldn't be too far away.'

'Right,' Caro said. 'Thanks.'

'Hello, Richard,' Vicki said. She looked at the policeman.

'Hello, Missus Robbins,' Richard said.

'How's Jennifer?'

'Good. Yeah, she's really good, thanks,' Richard said. 'And who's the young man?'

'That's Noah,' Caro said. 'Sophie's boyfriend.'

Noah looked down at his feet.

'He's a lovely boy,' Vicki said. 'Derek Hermann's son.'

'And what time are your parents expecting you?' Richard asked.

'They didn't say a time.' Caro could hardly hear him as he spoke.

'He's got four older sisters,' Vicki said. 'They probably think they've said it often enough.'

'Right,' Richard said. 'Well, I think it's time you were home. One of those cars out there yours?'

Noah nodded.

'We might just follow you home, I think.'

'Mum,' Sophie said, and looked at Caro, but Caro didn't say anything.

'Tell them not to follow him home,' Sophie said. 'There's no need. He didn't bring them here.'

Caro shrugged.

'I think it's time I left,' Vicki said.

The car doors banged, the engines started one by one.

Caro lit a cigarette. 'Just go to bed,' she said, and took a drag. 'It's half past three.'

Sophie didn't move. 'Mum.'

'I said go to bed.' Caro's words were sharp, and when Sophie went to speak, she held up her hand. 'I'm not interested and I don't want to hear,' she said. 'I told you to go.' She closed her eyes, waited until she could hear Sophie shuffling away. 'And don't forget to clean your teeth,' she called. Stupid words.

Sophie came back, leaned against the door. 'I didn't know where you were.' Black streaks ran down her face. 'I didn't know where you were. We didn't notice the time. I just didn't think. And then, I didn't know where you were.'

I was your age once, Caro thought. She rolled the cigarette between her fingers. I was your age, and I came home to an empty house. She had wanted to get Auntie Jess, but it was Aunt Dot who came.

The smoke was curling.

They wouldn't let her back in the house, and even Auntie Jess seemed to think that it was for the best.

Caro looked at Sophie and Sophie had never looked so much like Sean. The child her father left behind.

It won't hurt to let Sophie see you cry. It was Graeme who said that first. She brushed tobacco scraps from her lap and went to her child.

'Oh, sweetheart.' She put her arms around Sophie and held her to her chest. 'Oh, my darling, darling girl.'

She used a gentle mother's voice. She hugged her child and kissed her forehead, smoothed her hair.

Caro had not noticed before, but Sophie's hair was as soft as Sean's had been.

CHAPTER TWENTY-FIVE

Caro was half-expecting Vicki to drop in, and she decided she wouldn't have a drink until then. But when the, Hello? It's only me came, it was Libby.

'Hello, dear,' Libby said, when she appeared at the kitchen door. 'The door was open, so I let myself in.' Her hair was neat, she had lipstick on, and she carried a black handbag.

'I was just on my way home from book club. Jane Austen today. It was at Vera's, so I had to drive past, and I saw the car, and I thought . . . well, you're very hard to catch so I thought I'd just pop in.'

'Of course,' Caro said. 'It's lovely to see you.' She brushed quickly at her hair and her shirt and her pants.

Libby came to kiss her on the cheek and Caro offered the kissing noise back, although she missed Libby's cheek. Libby smelled of sweat.

'Would you like a gin?' Caro asked. 'I've got tonic. No brandy, I'm afraid.'

'Thank you. Today I think I will,' Libby said.

She watched as Caro poured.

'Is Sophie here?' Libby asked.

'No, you've missed her. She's gone to Emma's, but she'll be

back for tea. I've told her I'm making this.' She waved her arm across the bench, vegetables all laid out. 'Mise en place,' she said, and laughed. It was a very good joke to make at herself.

'Meez on what?' Libby said.

'Mise en place. It's what French chefs say. Everything's in place. You know, get everything ready before you start to cook.'

She laughed again, to show it was a joke. It was really very good.

'Oh,' Libby said. 'I wouldn't have thought that needs its own word.'

'Ice?' Caro asked.

'Yes please. I'll have mine on the rocks.'

Caro handed the drink to Libby, held hers in the air.

'Cheers,' she said.

'Good health,' said Libby.

Caro gulped and Libby sipped.

'I hope your drink's not too strong,' Caro said. She was suddenly embarrassed at its strength. After she had finished giving up smoking, then she would cut down on the drinks. Not give up, just cut down.

'No, no, it's fine,' Libby said. She held the glass with both hands wrapped around. There was a hole in her stockings, right down at the ankle. And a ladder moving up.

'I've given up smoking,' Caro said, pointing to the jar. 'I'm putting money in whenever I think I would have finished a packet.'

Libby looked at the jar. 'How long has it been?'

'Just this week.' Caro took a drink. 'You know what they say. Every journey begins with a single step.'

'You might put a couple more coins in,' Libby said. 'It's Thursday now.'

Libby took another sip and Caro took a slug.

'Why don't you have a seat?' Caro said. She waved her hand to the stool at the breakfast bar. 'I'll clear a space . . . goodness me . . . you'd think I hadn't cleaned for at least a year . . . and then you sit here, and if you don't mind, I'll keep cooking while we talk.' She balanced the coffee cups, the plate she had used for toast and the empty wine bottle, took them quickly to the sink.

'Of course, of course, you go ahead,' Libby said. 'Perhaps I shouldn't have come.'

'Oh no, you're very welcome. It's nice to have you here. It's just I promised Sophie I'd make minestrone and she was in such a good mood when she left and I don't want to let her down. You know what teenagers are like.' Caro sighed. 'I said what do you want for tea, and she said minestrone soup. Without the meat, of course. So I've got a tin of lentils here. And I said – although I don't know why – would you like dessert. I was thinking ice-cream, I suppose. And she said pudding with chocolate sauce. Pudding? We haven't had pudding for years. Pudding's a camping dessert.' She sighed. 'And we only ever have tinned.'

'Are you cooking more these days?' Libby asked.

'Well, yes, of course,' Caro said. 'Of course.'

Caro started with the mushrooms, because she couldn't

do onion in front of Libby. She pulled a handful from the bag, put them next to the chopping board. They had started to shrivel and dry. She couldn't sniff them in front of Libby, but they were only last week's. They should be okay.

'We're having lamb curry,' Libby said. 'It's all on plarse. I made it before book club. That's what I always do, that way if the discussion goes on, I don't have to start worrying what I'll give Joel for tea, you see, and then I'll heat it when Joel gets home – he always comes to me on Thursdays – and I just put the rice in a sieve and run hot water over it. It's so easy and that's what I like about curry,' she said. 'You should do more curry. You can do them on Sunday night and put them in the freezer. I suppose I should do some extra for you and bring them around.'

'That would be lovely,' Caro said. And it would. Libby was a brilliant cook, and wasn't that exactly the kind of thing she'd moved here for? To make the things between her and Libby simple and everyday. 'But don't forget. Sophie doesn't eat meat.'

'Oh, that,' Libby said. 'That's just a fad. I wouldn't be giving in to that.'

Libby clinked the ice in her glass, and Caro wished that it were Vicki sitting there.

Caro sliced the mushrooms thin, stalks on, because they looked so good that way once they were cooked.

'I heard you had the police around.'

'Well, kind of . . . not really . . . it was just a misunderstanding as it turns out.'

Caro used her knife to push the mushroom slices to the edge of the board.

'Do you like it here, Caroline? Are you enjoying living here?'

Enjoying?

'Because I'm wondering' – Libby's words followed on fast – 'why you're acting like this.'

Caro took a drink. 'Acting like what?' she asked. She didn't put her glass down and she still held on to the knife.

'You know what I mean,' Libby said. 'Pushing Heidi to fight for all these tests and things.'

Caro put down her drink, picked up another mushroom, waved the knife. 'It's part of my job. To find out what's wrong with people. To make them better.'

Caro sliced. She liked to get six slices from each mushroom.

'It's nothing new, you know,' Libby said. 'It's nothing that hasn't been said before.'

Caro heard Libby take another drink, put the glass back on the bench.

Slice, slice, slice, slice, slice.

'We're not stupid,' Libby said. 'We're not dumb.'

'Well, no, I never said you were.'

'Not in so many words,' Libby said. The ice rattled in her glass.

Caro put the knife down slowly, picked up her drink.

'Do you want Joel and Heidi to leave?' Libby said. 'Is that where this is going?'

'No,' she said. 'Course not. Not if they're happy here.'

Libby looked Caro in the eye. 'What happens when you leave?' she asked. 'To Heidi I mean? When you've pushed her into all of this . . . turned everyone against her . . .'

'I've decided to stay,' Caro said. 'Sophie and I have been talking about it quite a bit over the last few days. Staying would probably suit us both. At least for another year.'

They had talked about staying. They hadn't talked about Graeme.

Libby's ice rattled.

'Sophie's making friends, and I quite like my job,' Caro said. 'It does have its rewards.'

'Well, Joel will be pleased to hear that,' Libby said. 'He likes having you around.' She tipped the glass back as she drained the last of the drink. 'That's if he's still here.' She put the empty glass on the bench and picked up her bag. 'I'd better go, Joel will be wanting his curry. And you've still got pudding to do.'

She looked at her watch.

'You know, all my friends say imagine how hard it must be. Being a doctor. Trained to save people's lives. And watching your husband die.'

So here they finally were. In the place and the time that Caro had always known would arrive. She had waited for the words, they'd rattled around in her mind often enough. It would be good to have them out.

'I know what it's like to lose a husband,' Libby said.

Caro took another drink.

'You know when Tom died,' Libby said, 'I got eighteen

bunches of flowers. With Sean it was thirty-two. One hundred and sixty cards, I got. Six lasagnes in three days.'

'I didn't count our cards,' Caro said. 'Our house was full of flowers, but I didn't think to count.'

Libby looked at her watch again.

'I'd really better go.'

She turned and left. The back door closed with a click. Caro thought of running after her, or of opening the window and calling her back.

The conversation hadn't finished. There was still, If I'd been watching, I would have known. Just say it, Caro wanted to yell. Just get it over with.

Instead, Caro finished her drink, put down her glass, picked up the knife and started to slice. She liked the onion sliced in rings.

CHAPTER TWENTY-SIX

'So I've decided I will come.'

Heidi had practised the words all day and now she'd said them.

'To Queensland?' Mum said. 'To live?'

Heidi hadn't thought that Mum's surprise would sound so harsh.

'Yes. To live with you. Like you said.' My voice, Heidi thought, it's too frenzied.

'But you're having a baby, love.'

'I can have it there. You've got hospitals, haven't you?'

Mum didn't speak.

'Haven't you?' An accusation now.

'Well, yes, but . . . you've always said you wouldn't come.'

'I've changed my mind. I want to now.'

'Oh, love.'

'What?' Heidi asked again. 'What's wrong?'

'Oh, love. It's just . . . it wouldn't work . . . you couldn't live with me.'

'Why not? You said . . .' Heidi wished she didn't sound like she was eight years old. 'You asked me to come. It was your idea. You said.'

'Yes, but a baby, that changes things. I mean we wouldn't be able to concentrate. Not with a baby in the house.'

No. Mum was saying no.

'But I've already done the television show,' Heidi said. Her hand sweated around the phone. 'I told you. They've interviewed me! I can't stay here!'

'Oh, love,' Mum said. 'Don't let yourself run from them.'

In front of Heidi's eyes, the room was swimming. She closed her eyes tight until all she could see was black with orange lines.

'Heidi? Are you there?'

'Yes,' Heidi said. 'Of course I am.'

'I'm sorry, love, I don't want to sound . . .'

'Did you ever mean it? Did you ever mean I should come and live with you?'

There was nothing.

'You only said it cos you thought I wouldn't come,' Heidi said. She bit hard on her bottom lip. She would not cry.

'Oh, love,' Mum said.

'You told me . . . it was your idea . . . get Zac checked . . . write to the minister, send a letter to the company, it's their responsibility . . . take it to the school . . . I've done it all because you told me I should.'

'And you were right. You've acted the right way.'

'That's easy for you to say. You live up there. But this is my home. I have to live here.'

'I didn't tell you to go on television. You didn't ask me about that.'

Heidi thought about hanging up and never speaking to Mum again.

'Vicki Robbins rang me again.'

'So?' It was as if she were twelve again. Your teacher rang . . . So? . . . She said you weren't at school . . . So? . . . You'll be suspended if you do it again . . . So? So? So? Only Mum hadn't heard any of that, because Mum wasn't here when Heidi was twelve.

'You should let them see Zac,' Mum said.

'You've got no right,' Heidi said. 'You've got no more rights and I'm not listening to you.'

'I don't blame you. I don't. But I'm right about this. Take him over there. You won't lose anything.'

More silence.

'You know how Vicki Robbins got my number, don't you?'

More silence.

'Don't you think that tells you something?'

I will not speak.

'Look. I've got some money saved.' Her voice dropped even lower. 'Daniel doesn't know. It's yours. I'll send it to you. I'll put a cheque in the mail tomorrow. It'll help you move out of Dad's at least. Give you and Joel some privacy. A chance to sort your lives out.'

'Fuck off,' Heidi said, but still she didn't hang up. 'I don't want your cheque.'

Mum didn't say anything.

Heidi looked at her watch and wondered how long the silence could go.

CHAPTER TWENTY-SEVEN

Dad was still in the shower. If he didn't hurry it would start without him, and Heidi couldn't be sure she had the video set right. He had come straight home from work, not even gone for one drink, and they ate tea together, the two of them without Joel. Dad didn't ask, but Heidi told him anyway. Joel's gone up to his mum's, she had said.

Dad nodded and ate his chops with chips. Mouthful of chop, mouthful of chip, mouthful of chop.

Why did you do it? Joel had asked. Why did you let them interview you?

The journalist asked me, she had said.

You could have said no. You didn't have to go on TV.

It was true. She could have said no.

But the journalist had a nice voice. She made me feel good. Zac is sick. My baby might be too. These were things she couldn't say to Joel.

Heidi wouldn't have minded if Dad had stayed out too. It would have been good to sit down and watch it on her own first of all. To know the worst of how she looked. She couldn't remember a word she had said. It might be good to watch it alone.

But she couldn't be sure she'd get the video right.

Her stomach churned and she wished that Joel was here. Was an angry Joel better than no Joel at all? She twisted at her ring, rubbed the stone with her thumb, swung her legs up on to the lounge, let herself sink into the cushion. She liked the way it helped loosen her chest.

The packet of biscuits. There were only four left, and she had just bought them that afternoon. She took two for herself, left two for Dad.

Quarter past eight. If Dad was gonna see it, he needed to get out of the shower soon. And she still didn't know if the video was right. She finished the first biscuit, started on the second.

Dad's cup of tea would be cold.

She heard the shower turn off, listened to the clinks and the clunks as Dad dropped some things and put other things down.

Second biscuit, down the hatch.

She took a sip of her tea then put the cup down. Third biscuit. Dad would never know there had been four.

He came into the lounge room in his dressing gown and slippers.

'Can you check the video's right?' she said, and she watched as he fiddled with the remote. She held the biscuit, but did not bite. The video clunked and whirred.

'All systems go,' he said.

She took a bite from the biscuit. The music started. Her heart was thumping. She put the rest of the biscuit down.

They started with some guy in a white coat. He was sitting at a desk with shelves of books behind him.

'D'you know him?' Dad asked.

'No,' Heidi said.

'Looks like a bit of git, doesn't he?' Dad said.

'Shh,' Heidi said.

There was Caro. 'One of my patients brought her young child to me, and while she could not offer anything specific, she felt that there was something wrong. We ran a number of tests, none of which revealed anything. The mother of this child was adamant that we keep looking, and finally we found that the problem was lead.'

It was Mrs Maynard's turn. 'The mother of one of the children attending our school came to us and told us that her son had a blood lead level far in excess of that recommended by world health authorities. She was anxious to determine the cause of his high blood lead level and asked whether we would consider having an inspection of the site to identify any potential dangers. Naturally, we were concerned to ensure that our grounds and facilities were safe for all our children and we asked the local health officer for an audit of the site. The initial testing revealed that the soil of our community garden and the water in our rainwater tank both did, in fact, have higher levels of lead than they should.'

It sounded so simple when she heard Mrs Maynard saying it like that. It sounded so sensible. So controlled.

'Of course, we stopped the garden project straightaway, but we thought it would be prudent if all the children had their blood lead levels checked.'

'Lotta ladies, eh?' Dad said. 'Hadn't noticed that before. But there's a lot of ladies got involved.'

And then, there she was, walking down the footpath, Zac a little ahead on his bike while the journalist spoke over the top.

'Single mother Heidi Oswald, mother of the child concerned, spoke to the school council, asking them to request that all the children in the school have their blood lead levels tested,' the journalist said. 'Miss Oswald, whose only child Zac has recorded blood lead levels as high as thirty-two milligrams, has pursued testing for her own son ever since she noticed that something "wasn't right". She says that if there's a problem, parents have a right to know. Despite its resounding defeat, the proposal has remained a contentious topic of discussion and one which has the potential to divide the town. While there are some who quietly support Heidi Oswald's proposal, they are often reluctant to speak out, fearing a backlash from their family, friends and neighbours.'

And now there she was, her head taking up the whole screen, sitting in this very same chair, being shown to people all around Australia. The journalist was asking questions now.

'A lot of people I've spoken to today say that they don't think there's a problem here and that further testing isn't necessary. What's been your reaction to that?'

Heidi could see herself nodding to the journalist's question. Close-up like this she looked a real know-it-all.

'I know they're saying it, and a lot of them have said it to me.'

God, is that what she really sounded like? Like she was talking out of her *nose*.

'But this is about my little boy. And other children I might have.'

It was strange seeing herself rub at her stomach like that. She hadn't known that she got that look on her face.

'I just want to know that my children are safe, and that the places they play are safe.'

She still looked like a know-it-all, like she was trying to be somebody she wasn't. Like she was right and everybody else was wrong.

They were finished with her now, and there was a shot of the stack. It looked big when they showed it like that. Like it stretched over the whole town.

'The Port Joseph lead smelter is one of the largest in the world,' said the journalist. 'It directly employs about a quarter of the people who live in the town. But like all industry, it is a double-edged sword. Even with a number of significant improvements to the plant, emissions from the smelter continue. Recent investigations show that the levels of lead in the town's environment may be unacceptably high, leaving the residents of Port Joseph – particularly its children – exposed to a potentially dangerous situation.'

Back to the man in the white coat now. Heidi noticed now that he had copper-red hair, and was wearing glasses and a tie.

'Young children certainly have an increased risk of exposure to lead,' he said. 'They are more likely to bite their nails, to put contaminated objects in their mouths, and to eat sand or dirt. At the same time, younger children absorb lead more easily and are at a more crucial stage of mental and physical development. So yes, in terms of environmental lead pollution, we are primarily concerned with the population of young children in Port Joseph.'

The journalist was talking again.

'Eighty-five years ago, this land was donated to the town by the then owners of the smelters. The employees of the smelters built a playground for the town's children. With everyone pitching in, it took just two days. All the materials – including the soil needed for the paths – were donated by the smelters.'

'I didn't know that, did you?' Heidi asked.

Dad shrugged, and she couldn't tell whether he meant yes or no.

'Today,' said the journalist, 'the soil in this playground has been shown to have unusually high levels of lead. It's just one of the many places around the town that experts say can pose a real hazard to young children. And people like Heidi agree.'

There she was at the playground with Zac. There was a quick shot of the other kids who had been in the playground at the same time. There was Jac with Cindy, sitting in the sandpit. Cindy sucked on her fingers, then waved her hands in the air.

They were back in the lounge room now, and there was Heidi nodding again.

'Yeah, you know what kids are like. You give them a bath, but they're never clean and they're always putting stuff in their mouth. Yeah, I do worry about that. But I keep the house clean and dusted and mopped. And I try to stop Zac putting things in his mouth. Especially dirt and sand and stuff like that.'

There were more shots of the town, of people talking, but Heidi was thinking of the words she had said, the way they had put them together, to make it look like she was saying things she hadn't really meant.

'Well,' Dad said. 'That's that.'

'Fuck,' Heidi said.

It had looked like she was saying that Cindy was dirty. It looked like she was saying Jac shouldn't have let her do that. But you can't stop Cindy, Heidi knew that. Cindy's just one of those kids. You can't stop her putting sand in her mouth.

Dad was still looking at the television.

'Youse are gonna get more shit tomorrow, aren't you?' she said. 'At work I mean.'

'Yeah,' Dad said. 'We are.'

Heidi wondered whether Joel had watched it after all. Him and Libby sitting together on the lounge. 'I shouldn't have done it,' she said.

Dad hadn't touched his cup of tea.

'But I'm right,' she said. 'We should know. If it's our kids, then we should know.'

The television was too loud. She felt tired, wanted to be alone. 'I'm gonna go to bed,' she said. 'I'll see you tomorrow.'

She pushed herself off the lounge, picked up the cups and took them to the kitchen sink.

In Zac's room, she smoothed his hair with her palm,

rubbed his face with the back of her hand. 'I love you,' she whispered. 'I love you, my beautiful boy.'

She loved the curve of his fingers and the smooth skin on the back of his hand.

She pulled lightly at the blanket, smoothed it around his shoulders. She leaned over again and, just before she kissed him, breathed in the smell of his sleep.

'I love you.' She thought of picking him up, carrying him with her to her bed the way she used to do. He won't remember those nights, she thought. Even if I tell him, he won't remember them.

Heidi went into the bathroom and washed her face, combed her hair, brushed her teeth. She did not look at herself in the mirror while she brushed. She did not take her make-up off.

Pink pyjamas, lamp on, big light off, open the book, put it down, lamp off.

She might have felt the baby fluttering, but Heidi felt alone in the dark.

CHAPTER TWENTY-EIGHT

Heidi was standing at the gate when the siren sounded for the end of the shift. It would be another fifteen minutes at least before the first of them came out. You couldn't have a shower and get dressed in much less time than that. She was the only one waiting.

She looked over the boom gate and along the wide concrete path. The thin pine trees weren't as neat as they used to be, but the flower pots were new.

Sometimes, when she was little, she and Mum had come to wait for Dad. There was no wire fence back then, and all the wives and all their kids stood over on that side underneath the jacaranda trees. In those days, Mum wore lipstick in the same pale shade as everybody else's mum.

Heidi had liked to watch for people in the windows on the upstairs floor. A man in a white shirt walking past or looking out and stretching his arms. There were rows of folders on the ledge at the other end and a pile of books that never seemed to be used. From time to time, there was a bunch of flowers in one of the middle windows. Carnations mostly. Roses sometimes. Always white.

Which one is Dad's window? Heidi had asked Mum.

He hasn't got a window.

How do you know?

I just do. They wouldn't have windows where Dad works.

Does Dad have a window now? Heidi wondered. It wasn't the kind of question she could ask Dad or Joel.

Clarrie Henderson was in the sentry box today, sitting on the high swivelling chair. Heidi still missed Barry Smith in the sentry box. He used to let the kids look in, and sometimes he gave out musk sticks, while the mothers nodded and smiled and said, Well, you're very lucky, and, What do you say?

Clarrie slid the window open. He had the racing station playing. Under starter's orders.

'You can't stand there,' he said, and pointed at the 'Keep Clear' sign. 'You'll have to move.' They were racing. Clarrie slid the window closed.

Cars had started to pull up now. Barbi Bannister got out of her stupid little red car. That car would be useless with kids, but she had them all in there, bouncing around. Barbi looked at Heidi, but walked to Tanya Jewell's car without even giving Heidi a wave. Barbi always was a stuck-up bitch.

Heidi shivered. The shadows had already grown and it was still cold if you weren't in the sun. She moved out of the tree's shadow, shivering even as her body warmed. It was another beautiful clear day. If it keeps up like this, she thought, it'll be perfect for the grand final on Saturday. Heidi let herself imagine the end of the game and the moment when the whistle blew and throwing her arms in the air. I'm playing, she'd told Joel. My girls are gonna win and the A grade's gonna win too. The baby will be fine. One more week won't hurt.

The first of the men were coming out now, bags in their hands if they were walking, on their backs if they had bikes. Clarrie lifted the boom and waved every now and then, but he didn't open his window again. As they passed her, some of the guys looked at her and some of them said hi, but most of them looked away or pretended they hadn't seen her.

She waved at Joel when she saw him coming down the path. He did not smile, even as he reached her, but he did lean towards her and he did kiss her cheek. She had not been expecting a kiss, not in front of everyone. His lips were cool, and she shivered inside. She wanted him to kiss her again, but properly this time, not just hello, and if he did, she would kiss him back.

She nodded towards the boom gate and the path. 'D'you know I've never been in there? All these years and I've never been closer than this or out along the wharf.'

Joel looked along the path, then turned back to Heidi. 'What are you doing here?'

It was a fair enough question. She was not one of the ones who usually came to the gate. She didn't even have the car.

'I was just out for a walk,' she said. 'And then I realised the time, and thought I could come and meet you.'

'I run on Thursdays,' Joel said. 'I've got my running gear on.' He held his arms out at his side as if to show her, as if she hadn't seen. It was strange to see him in his running gear when he smelled so fresh and looked so clean. But they had to have showers before they left the plant.

'Oh,' she said. 'Yes. I forgot. Hormones, I guess. I just wanted to see you, that's all.'

He looked around again, sighed. 'I'll have to go for a run after tea,' he said. 'It's a big game this weekend. I have to train.'

His hair had grown too long. She wished he would let it grow properly long again so it wouldn't matter so much the time he left between haircuts.

'Where's Zac?'

'With Renee.'

Joel's hand in hers was rough and dry. She had told him to use moisturiser, but she knew he never would.

'So how was your day?' he asked.

There was no smell of aftershave. Didn't he usually splash it on after every shower? Even if he didn't shave?

'It was okay. Didn't do much. I was pretty tired. How about you?'

'Okay. It was just work.'

He dropped her hand. Ten more steps and then I'll tell him, she thought. No. Still too many people around. When we get past the museum, I'll tell him then.

But they were past the museum and the post office and the old customs house and the library, and still neither of them had said a word.

She had always liked the way the main road curved like that. She liked that there were two lanes running either way, a flag-studded median strip separating them. She liked the sounds the flag ropes made against the poles. She couldn't tell him here, not in the middle of the shops. She looked ahead. It wouldn't take them long to get up to South Terrace. Another five minutes wouldn't matter.

Hi, Joel. G'day, Joel. How's it going, Joel? They were people who knew her too, but she was getting used to being ignored. She fitted her feet into the diamond pavers as they walked. Step on a crack and you break your mother's back. Walking in the sunshine, sing a little sunshine song. Who's tripping down the streets of the city. They were the songs that her and Mum would sing when they walked Dad home.

Without looking up, she knew exactly where they were. Kids' clothes, newsagent, jewellers, dry cleaner. Cross the road. Florist, photographer, empty shop, no more shops.

They turned right at South Terrace.

They would be home soon.

'I wanna leave,' she said. She swallowed after she spoke then licked her lips. She'd forgotten to put on lipstick before she left the house.

'What do you mean? Leave what?'

She watched the footpath as she walked, unable look at Joel.

'Leave here. I wanna go and live somewhere else. I want to go,' she said and made each word sound clear. 'I want to leave Port Joseph. Find somewhere else to live.'

'Where? Where do you wanna go?' His words were quick and sharp.

'I dunno.' She shrugged. 'It doesn't have to be Adelaide. Port Lincoln, maybe? Wallaroo? Somewhere without any lead.'

He stopped walking. She had to stop too, and she had to look at him.

'There's problems everywhere,' he said. 'Nowhere's perfect.'

She followed him.

'Zac is sick. And the baby might be too.' The words sounded bare, like she was blaming him. He slowed down and looked around. She wasn't surprised that he didn't speak.

'So what do you think?' she said.

'About what?'

'About moving away.'

'You know I can't leave Mum.'

He was walking too fast, but she made herself keep up.

'What about me? And the baby? And Zac?' She didn't know what else to say.

'You're the one changing the rules,' he said.

'It's not a game. We don't have any rules.'

He did not speak for another twenty-four steps.

'I *love* you,' he said.

'I know,' she said. 'That's why I want you to come.'

'You're gonna leave even if I stay, aren't you?'

'Yes.' This was the part she had not practised in her head.

He was walking too fast again, too fast for her to keep up.

'I know how Vicki Robbins got Mum's phone number.' That wasn't in her plan. She hadn't planned to let him know she knew that Vicki Robbins had asked him, that he'd agreed to pass the number on.

He stopped, turned around.

'When are you going?' he asked.

'As soon as I can.'

'Before the baby comes?'

'I want to leave next week. After the grand final.'

'This is bullshit, Heidi,' he said, then he stopped again. So did she. When he put his hands on her shoulders, she was surprised they felt so light.

'I'm supposed to be a dad,' he said.

'You will be.'

'I really want that baby.'

His fringe was too long. He should get it cut before he played on Saturday.

She did not want his hands on her shoulders anymore, but she did not want to push them away. Goosebumps crept down her arms.

'You can have the baby,' she said. 'You just can't have it if you live here.'

'I wouldn't leave you,' he said.

He dropped his hands, but she felt their pressure still.

'I can't give you anymore,' she said.

'Think I will run after all,' Joel said, his eyes were not quite blank. 'Don't hold tea for me. I'll eat at Mum's.'

He turned and started to run.

CHAPTER TWENTY-NINE

'Joel won't be home for tea,' Heidi said. 'He's gone to his mum's. He'll probably stay the night.'

'Right,' Dad said.

Heidi put the dinner on the table. Sausages, mashed potatoes, carrots and peas. With bread of course. Dad and Zac first, then hers.

She took the sauce from the cupboard.

'Bought,' she said. 'There's none of this year's homemade left.' Dad sniffed, but he poured a huge circle onto his plate.

She sat next to Zac.

'Salt?' Dad asked.

'Sorry. I forgot.' She clapped her hand to her forehead. 'Forget my head if it wasn't screwed on.' She got up again, took the salt and the pepper from the cupboard, put it on the side of the table as she walked past.

Dad stretched across the table to reach it and Heidi sat down, picked up her knife and fork.

She cut the end from her sausage, put it in her mouth.

'I want sauce,' Zac said.

'What do you say?' she said through her mouthful of food.

'Pleease,' he said.

'Can you pass the sauce please, Dad?' she asked, because he hadn't even moved. He pushed it across without looking up. 'Thanks.' She squeezed some onto Zac's plate, then hers. She got another slice of sausage in her mouth.

'Can I have a drink?' Zac said.

'In a minute,' she said. She scraped some potato onto her fork.

'I'm thirsty now,' he said, a whine in his voice.

'I'm eating my tea. Can't you wait?'

'But I'm so thirsty. I can't eat when I'm thirsty.'

She put the potato in her mouth, put down her knife and fork, stood up. 'Okay. What do you want, water or milk?'

'Milk,' he said. 'I want milk.'

'What do you say?' she asked.

'Pleeeease.'

She got the milk from the fridge, undid the lid, took a sniff.

'No. Not milk. Water. I want water,' Zac said.

She put the milk on the bench, walked to the sink, turned on the tap.

'No. Not water. Milk.'

'Which is it?' she snapped. 'What do you want? Make up your mind.'

'Milk. Pleeease.'

She took the cup of milk to the table, put it next to Zac and sat back down. 'I went to the doctor again yesterday.'

Zac picked up the cup. 'Use two hands,' she told him.

Zac put the cup back on the table and Heidi reached out automatically to move it away from his elbow.

'Zac isn't getting any better,' she said. 'His latest results were the worst they've ever been.'

Dad's knife squeaked along his plate making Heidi clench her teeth. Dad put another piece of sausage in his mouth.

'It's five months in a row now that his levels have gone up,' she said. 'And before that, they never went down. The best they ever do is stay the same. So they've gone up overall.'

Dad pushed a forkful of carrot into his mouth. Filled his fork with potato and held it while he chewed, his mouth not quite closed. He swallowed, opened his mouth, put the potato in.

Zac's plate fell on the floor with a bang. She didn't have to look to know. Mashed potato cowpat and splashes of sauce.

'Oh, Zac,' she said. She put her head in her hand.

Zac started to cry.

'It's just an accident. I'm sorry, Mum.'

'I know, I know. It's okay, sweetie,' she said. 'Here. You have mine.' She cut her sausage into small pieces, pushed her plate towards him. 'Here you go.'

'I want mine.' Zac cried and pointed to the floor.

'That's all yucky now. I'll clean it up. You just eat mine,' she said.

'No. Mine,' he said and shook his head roughly.

'You can't, sweetie,' she said. 'I told you. It's all yucky.'

'I want mine!' He was shouting now.

'For God's sake, just give it to him,' Dad said. 'He's only going to eat one more piece. It won't kill him.'

'No,' she said. 'He's not eating food that's fallen on the floor.'

She bent down, scraped what she could back to the plate and took it to the bin.

Zac cried and yelled. Dad stood up from the table, left the kitchen, his plate still on the table. There were only carrots left.

Heidi covered her face with her hands. Then she looked at Zac and smiled. 'Want some ice-cream?'

He was looking at her, but he was still crying.

'You can have Milo on top,' she said.

She sat with him while he ate. The ice-cream covered his chin, ran over his shirt, dripped on the table. More slimy spills to wipe up. She used the heels of her hands to rub hard at her eyes, enjoying the spots and stripes the pressure made.

'It's all right, Mummy,' Zac said.

She looked up, propped her hands under her chin.

'I know, sweetheart,' she said. She gave him a smile and he gave her a grin. God he looked like Brad. She reached over to brush the back of her fingers against his cheeks. Zac kept eating and Heidi couldn't stop herself from thinking it again. What if beautiful eyes were enough?

'Can I have some more?' Zac asked and held his bowl out to her. 'Pleease. More pleease.'

'Sure,' she said. 'Then it's time to get ready for bed.'

Teeth, toilet, bed. That's what Mum had always said, and it sounded simple like that. But there were bath, pyjamas, a story, a song, then bed. And then one more song and one more kiss and one more snuggly. Please.

Heidi sat at the kitchen table after it had all been done. She looked at the clock. And before you know it, it's half past eight, the day's already gone and there's still dishes on the table.

If she left tonight, she could leave the lot behind. Not even move them to the sink. Is that what happened to Mum? Was it the dishes? The ironing? The bath that had to be scrubbed? Had it been as simple as that?

Heidi put on the kettle and cleared the table while it boiled. She made two cups of tea, stirred sugar into one. She put biscuits on plates, the plates and the cups on a tray and carried the tray into Dad.

Would she miss all of this, she wondered. How would it be to live in another house?

'The doctor's been testing my blood too. Because of the baby.' She may as well tell him everything now.

'Right,' Dad said.

'It's five months in a row that Zac's levels have gone up. And now my levels are going up too. It's bad for the baby.'

She was determined not to cry.

Dad picked up his cup of tea. It rattled against the saucer.

'We're gonna move,' Heidi said. 'Zac and me. We're going away.'

Dad's eyes did not move away from the television.

'Joel has to decide whether he's going to come,' Heidi said. She lifted her fingers, felt for the ring with her thumb.

'Would you have gone?' It was the first time she had ever asked out loud. 'If Mum had asked you, would you have gone with her?'

'I dunno.' Dad shrugged.

Heidi kept twisting the ring.

'Is it true she didn't ask you if you wanted to go with her?'

'It was a long time ago,' Dad said.

'Brad's back again. I'm gonna see him tomorrow. And I'm gonna see his mum and dad.'

Dad looked at her.

'I'm gonna talk to them about them seeing Zac every now and then. If that's what they want. Just every now and then.'

Dad didn't say anything.

'It's not right, keeping them away from Zac like that,' she said. 'If they want to see him, they can. You only get one dad. And he should have a gran.'

'What difference does it make now?' Dad asked. 'If you're gonna leave anyway?'

Heidi could hardly breathe. 'We'll work something out,' she said.

Dad dunked his biscuit, then sucked on it. He slurped at his tea and turned the television up.

CHAPTER THIRTY

'Here he is,' Vicki said. She stood just behind Zac, her arm around the back of his neck, her hand on his shoulder. 'This is Zac. Zac . . . this is Brad.'

Caro stood in the doorway of the lounge room, Sophie behind her, not sure what she was supposed to be doing now that they had delivered Zac safely here. If the introductions weren't her job, then what was? Was she supposed to be staying closer to Zac, making sure that . . . making sure that what? That no one else touched him, that no one else told him who he was, who Brad was, who Robbo was. Caro didn't even know what the boy had been told about today. About anything. She should have asked, but she hadn't thought about it all. She had just blindly agreed when Heidi said, If I let Zac see them, will you go with him?

What had she been thinking about when Heidi asked her to do this? The next appointment probably. Or Sophie's subject choices for next year, no chemistry, no physics, but both drama and art. Or the flowers Graeme had started sending every Tuesday afternoon and the calls he made every second night, and what Sophie might have overheard. Whatever it was, whatever she'd been thinking about, she should have listened more closely to Heidi, and she should have been thinking about Heidi and Zac and Brad.

Caro watched now as Brad held his hand out to the little boy. With only a small hesitation, Zac put his hand in Brad's. Brad let his large hand close over the little boy's, then shook it gently up and down.

'Pleased to meet you,' Brad said. His voice was deeper than it was strong.

If Caro had ever stopped to form a picture of Brad, he wouldn't have looked like the man she saw now. Tanned perhaps, but never that tall and never that thin. From the photo on Vicki's desk, she knew that his hair was black, but she would not have imagined the ponytail which he wore, as men who had ponytails did, with the band where the base of his head met the top of his neck. He wore black leather strips plaited around one wrist and on the other, a coloured friendship band. His feet were bare and he had a tattoo on his ankle.

To the extent that she had ever thought about Brad at all, it had been as Vicki's son or Heidi's ex-boyfriend. A character in other people's lives. And yet, here he was, a full-grown man complete with three-day growth.

Caro thought, I bet he doesn't smoke.

His knees cracked loudly in the quiet room as he squatted down and looked at Zac more carefully. 'I've heard a lot about you,' he said. He still held Zac's hand in his. 'And I've been wanting to meet you for a very long time.' Brad's smile was quick and uncertain.

Caro thought that even if she could see Zac's face, she

would not see a smile, but she could not be sure. He had not taken his hand away from Brad's.

'And this is my dad,' Brad said, gesturing across the room. 'You can call him Robbo if you like. That's what all his friends call him. Even me and my sister, Helen, call him Robbo.'

Zac still did not speak, but he let Brad guide him over to Robbo sitting in the corner chair – a recliner, probably bought in the last few months, and the footrest almost permanently out – his dressing gown pulled around his body and held in place with a tasselled cord.

Robbo looked even paler than he had last week, Caro thought. Well, they called it pale, but pale was a euphemism. Robbo looked grey. His weight was falling away and his hair would never grow back now. He lifted his arm in a wave at Zac and his smile was not as weak as it might have been.

'Hello, young man,' Robbo said. 'Thank you for visiting us.' His voice had only a hint of a rasp today, and his eyes were focused on Zac.

'You're welcome,' Zac said. He pushed his hands into his pockets as he spoke, but then he added, 'It's nice to meet you, Robbo.'

There was a twang in Zac's voice – a child's voice with an adult's lilt – that made Caro want to laugh and say, Isn't that cute. But then, Robbo wiped at his eyes, first with his hand, then with a tissue which he took from the box on the coffee table next to his chair.

Caro could feel Sophie's restlessness growing behind her, but she still didn't know what to do. Should she introduce herself to Brad? Should she peck Robbo on the cheek like she would usually do? Should she sit or stand, stay or leave?

'Shall I put the kettle on?' she asked, but as soon as she did, she wished that she hadn't spoken. It hadn't been her silence to break.

'Oh. Thank you. Yes, that would be lovely,' Vicki said. She did not look away from Zac as she spoke.

'I'll do it,' Sophie said. 'You go and sit down, Mum.'

'Oh. Well, I'll help you, shall I?' She made her voice as light as Sophie's had been.

'I said I'll do it.' Now, Sophie clipped the end of every word.

How had Caro forgotten the pattern of this conversation? They'd had it every day for months, several times a day. And it was no more than eighteen months since they'd stopped.

She shouldn't have let Sophie come with her today. When Sophie had said, last night as they talked about it over tea, I'll come, Caro should have thought less about having an extra person there and more about what Sophie would see. Caro should have thought about this room and how familiar it would be. Familiar, but without a hint of nostalgia. Not so different to their own front room of eighteen months ago, tidied, quiet and light, the man in the corner opening his eyes for minutes at a time, his shallow, irregular breaths marking time and always filled with friends who knew they shouldn't come, but who couldn't stay away.

And the closer he got to the end, the more the friends would come and the longer they would sit.

Caro remembered herself, sitting awkwardly, not knowing

what to do with any of them. It only took minutes to tell them what she knew. Maybe two more weeks, she would say. The next few days. It could be anytime. He's comfortable. He ate breakfast this morning. He slept well last night. She could tell them the drugs that he'd taken, the drugs that he'd stopped, and the ones she had thought of putting him on. Sedatives, anti-nausea, pain relief. She told them all these things, and they would nod at appropriate times, but she could never tell them enough. They were always holding their breath or clearing their throat or crossing their arms against their chests, as if all of her endings were commas and they never heard the full stops.

Caro had never understood the way they thought, these friends of Sean's. Teachers, all of them, and yet still they seemed to think that every problem could be solved. They seemed so full of expectation. As if one day she would open the door and say: Good news! It's not as bad as we thought. The tumour's shrunk. They've found a cure.

Had they always been like that and she had never noticed, or was it just their way of thinking through unmapped times like these?

And while she had been kept busy finding new ways to say old things, Sophie seemed to know, just as Sean had done, when to offer beer and when to offer tea. Who had milk in their coffee and who drank chamomile. She knew, like Sean had known, when ginger biscuits worked and when it was time for olives and crackers and cheese.

Once Caro had noticed, she had tried to stop it of course

she had, but Sophie had pushed her away. It's all right. I can do it. Mum. Please. Just sit down. She clipped her words and rounded out her sentences with short, impatient sighs. Caro's sighs, not Sean's.

'Look over here, Zac. I've got some lego out for you.' Vicki pointed to the small table against the wall. 'It was Brad's when he was a boy.'

Libby could do that too. Pull her children's things out of cupboards or from boxes under beds. She had Sean's first cardigan, his first pair of shoes, a pull-along toy with the paint worn off the wheels. Libby was always finding something – a school book, a newspaper clipping, a swimming trophy – and handing it to Caro with the same introduction: I thought you'd like to see this.

'Yeah, I used to love lego. Do you like lego, Zac?' Brad asked.

Zac nodded.

'Oh, well, come and look, I've got some road and some train tracks, and there's a crane you can make, and I've still got the rope for the winch.'

'Cool,' Zac said, with more feeling in his voice than Caro had ever heard from him before. He and Brad sat down at the table together and the lego rattled and clicked as they started to sort the pieces.

Vicki was sitting next to Robbo now, holding his hand and using her other to rub gently on his arm. Now that she saw them all together in the same room, Caro could see what Vicki meant – that Zac looked like Brad, and Brad looked like

Robbo. Which meant that Zac looked like Robbo and Robbo looked like him.

Sophie brought in cups of tea one by one, Robbo's first, moving his coffee table closer to his chair, making sure he could reach the cup, that it wouldn't be too hot, that she had the milk done right, even though she must know that Robbo wouldn't drink it in the end.

After the cups of tea, Sophie brought in biscuits on a plate which she offered around the room. Sophie had grown used to her height these days, Caro thought, and carried it more gracefully. Her back more straightened, her shoulders less slumped. And her hair did look gorgeous cut that way. It seemed to take an hour every morning in the bathroom. But it meant that her eyes were no longer hidden under her fringe.

'These are delicious,' Caro said. 'Is that orange-chocolate icing?'

'I think so,' Vicki said. 'Helen made them. She just dropped them around this morning. Her kids love them, so she thought Zac might too.'

Caro looked at Sophie, handing the plate around for the second time. 'These biscuits *are* good,' she said. 'I'll have to get the recipe from Helen, won't I, Mum?'

Was that the kind of daughter Sophie wanted to be? Making biscuits for her mother and even after she'd left home still dropping them around. Did Sophie want to be like Helen who rang her mother two, three, four times every day, dropping by on her way to the supermarket just to ask, Do you need bread or milk?

With Noah on the sidelines, it might be only steps away, that kind of life. Already they had plans for his parents' Yorke Peninsula shack on New Year's Eve and even Easter. Easter was more than six months away. Sophie was only fifteen, but she had the kind of boyfriend who made plans for six months' time.

It would keep Caro awake again tonight, going back over her lists of reasons to leave and her reasons to stay, her reasons to be with Graeme and her reasons to be alone.

Maybe it would be fun. Maybe Sophie could be that kind of daughter and she could be that kind of Mum. Just drop the kids around, they can stay the night, you sleep in, pick them up at lunchtime if you like.

She could hear Sean laughing at her now. The out loud laugh he'd used when she had said, one New Year's Eve, I'm going to run a marathon this year. A marathon? he'd said. It was not a laugh he had ever used before.

Zac was shaking his head at the biscuits Sophie offered him.

'Would you like an ice-cream instead?' Vicki asked.

Zac looked to Caro. 'Can I?' he asked.

'Of course you can, sweetheart,' she said. Sweetheart? Had she ever used the word before? And why had he looked to her? What authorities had Heidi told him that Caro had been given?

'We've got chocolate or strawberry. Or both. You can have both if you like.'

'Ummmm . . .' Zac said.

'Why don't you come with me and have a look?' Vicki said.

They left the room together, Vicki saying, 'And we've got hundreds and thousands too. Hundreds and thousands or chocolate sauce. And you can have it in a bowl or in a cone.'

The room was even more quiet now. Quiet enough to notice the birds, the car going slowly down the road, and the radio out there somewhere in another room.

'How long are you home for, Brad?' Caro asked. What a stupid question.

'They've given me leave without pay,' Brad said. 'They'll hold my job open for me.'

'Oh, that's good.'

'But we'll see what happens, I guess, maybe I'll stay in Adelaide.'

He raised his voice in a question, but what could Caro tell him?

She knew the answer, because Heidi had told her, I'm gonna leave next week. I'm gonna live in Adelaide.

I'll miss you, Caro had said.

Will you?

Of course. It had just been something to say, but she meant it all the same. She had even thought of giving Heidi a hug.

We could catch up next year, Heidi had said. When you've moved back to Adelaide.

We're not moving back. Not yet. We're staying here.

But you said . . . I thought . . . you're only here for a year.

'Brad's been teaching at a school in Thailand,' Caro told Sophie now.

'Yeah, I know,' she said. 'You already told me that.'

'Do you like it?' Caro asked, turning back to Brad.

'I love it,' he said. 'I wish Zac could meet those kids. They're gorgeous. They've got nothing like this,' he said, pointing at the lego, 'But they just laugh all day. They laugh at me all the time. Especially when I try and speak Thai.'

You wanted him to bring his photos out, Caro thought. You would sit as he flicked through them and said things like, It was just the most amazing day, they're lovely people, so gentle and kind. Even his cliches would make your heart race.

And now she remembered one of the things that Heidi had said.

Will you go with Zac? I can't trust myself to go.

'Do you know what you're going to do after you've finished school?' Brad was looking at Sophie.

'I'm gonna be an actor,' she said.

Robbo gave a small cough, shifted a little in his seat, but soon closed his eyes again.

'Actually,' Brad went on, 'I really wanted to be a doctor, but I didn't get the marks.'

Caro had a standard answer, delivered in a standard tone. 'Really?'

'Yeah. I thought about repeating, but then . . . that didn't work out, and I thought teaching might be good.'

He reminded Caro of Sean. In the back of his eyes, his fidgeting fingers, his unsaid words, he reminded Caro of Sean.

'Is he really sick? Zac I mean. Is it as serious as Heidi says it is?'

'I'm not allowed . . .'

'No. I'm sorry, I shouldn't have said anything. Mum warned me. I'm just trying to understand why Heidi's the only one who's scared.'

Look around you! Caro wanted to shout. Why is this so bloody hard? She's not the only who's scared. There's others. She's just the only who's brave enough to say she's scared.

'But she's right if she's thinking of moving?'

I would. If it were me, with a little kid, living in a house at that end of town, I would. I'd move.

'I can't . . .'

Robbo started to cough again now. A heaving, but shallow cough, as if he couldn't get the breath to make it work.

'You okay, Dad?' Brad jumped from his seat, grabbing the tissue box from the coffee table next to his father's chair, standing at his side, handing him a tissue, all in one smooth move.

His father nodded.

'You sure?' There was an edge in Brad's voice. 'Do you need anything? A drink?'

Robbo shook his head, but he kept coughing, filling the tissues from his chest, handing them to Brad, taking a new one. When he stopped coughing, he let his head fall against the chair, his eyes closed. His arms had fallen to his side, but he still held a tissue in one hand. Brad stood, awkwardly now, at the side of his father's chair.

Sophie had her hands in her lap and was looking down at them, twisting her fingers, picking at her fingernails then twisting her fingers again.

'Oh.' Caro grabbed at her bag, then patted at her pocket. 'I've just realised, I've left my pager at home . . . would you mind going home to get it, Sophie?'

'You're not on call,' Sophie said.

'No, but I've got a few patients who might need me this weekend. I like to have it with me anyway.'

'Okay,' Sophie said. She held out her hand and Caro dropped the keys into her palm.

'Can you check the washing machine while you're there? If it's finished, you can hang that load out.'

'Do you need your pager or not?'

How many mistakes am I supposed to let her make?

'Once you've got the pager, then if it goes off, you can come and get me.'

'Okay. I'll see you later, Mister Robinson,' Sophie said, her voice only slightly raised. 'It was good to meet you.' She moved towards his chair, leaned down and kissed his forehead. He opened his eyes and looked at her as she stood again.

'Thank you,' Robbo said.

And in the moments it took for Sophie to turn and sweep her hair behind her ears and say goodbye to Brad and leave only her perfume in the room, Caro realised she had her answer for Sean's New Year's laugh.

She didn't want to run a marathon. She just wanted to be the kind of person who could.

CHAPTER THIRTY-ONE

'You shouldn't be so worried,' Caro said. 'You'll win.'

'Really?' Sophie said. 'D'you really think?'

'I know you will. I've got a *feeling* about it.'

'I didn't know you had feelings.'

Caro laughed. 'I don't very often,' she said. 'But when I do they're always right.'

'They've started warm-ups,' Sophie said, 'I have to go.' She ran ahead.

The fold-up chair banged against Caro's legs and because they were almost late and the car park was almost full, she had the longest walk of anyone. But still she was pleased with herself for not forgetting the chair. The chair, a wide-brimmed hat, sunscreen, a drink for Sophie, and even a drink for herself.

The complex looked different today with only a few of the courts being used, but all of those with crowds on all four sides.

Caro found the right court, and as soon as they saw her, the other mums shuffled themselves around, saying, No, that's fine, there's plenty of room, here you are, put your chair here. And only one of them looked away just as Caro smiled.

The umpires – dressed in white and plumper above the knees than they might once have been – checked the small gold watches they wore rested on their breasts. They nodded to each other, then one of them blew her whistle and waved the girls into facing lines.

The girls held their hands palms out and the umpires moved, girl by girl, along the lines, stopping sometimes to rub at a girl's finger tops or to lift her hair further from her ears, checking for nails that hadn't been shortened or earrings that weren't removed.

Emma's getting her ears pierced next week, Sophie had said. Once netball's finished.

Is she?

She said we should go together. We should get them done at the same time.

Did she?

So can I? Can I get my ears pierced? When Emma does hers?

Caro had said no, but she didn't mean it and the next time Sophie asked, Caro would say, Yes. She might even just say, out of the blue, after tea tonight perhaps, You can get your ears pierced if you like. I'll pay.

An umpire handed a coin to Emma, Emma tossed it and the Magpies' captain called. 'Tails.'

The three of them – Emma, the Magpies' captain, the umpire dressed in white – leaned in as the coin fell to the ground.

'Heads,' the umpire said. 'United? Pass or end?'

Heidi waved the girls into their positions then walked off the court, took her place amongst the mothers, called out

'Okay, United' and clapped her hands once. 'We should win it,' she said. 'We should.' Lucy's mother patted her arm and another mother Caro didn't recognise leaned over from two seats down and gripped Heidi's knee. 'We'll be right,' the mother said, her knuckles white.

There was a man on the other side of the court with a cigarette in his hand. A father. Sean would have come too. But if Sean had come, then she wouldn't have.

United got the first two goals, gave the next two away, but got the next three.

'Good work, Sophie,' Caro said, when Sophie stopped a centre pass. 'Keep it going, United,' she called, when they got a goal. 'Take this one back, United,' she yelled, when the other team scored. She was surprised at the strong thuds of her heart and the clenching of her teeth.

She could really do with a fag.

They were up at quarter time, up at half time, but the scores were level at the three-quarter break. Heidi stood on the court, the girls clustered around her. They sucked on the orange quarters that Suzie Woolf handed around and Lucy's mother poured them a final round of drinks from the chipped foam cask. The girls' eyes followed Heidi's gestures from one end of the court to the other. She put her arms around the two closest girls, and they all leaned in towards her, giving nods that were earnest beyond their years.

The umpire blew the whistle. One minute and the last quarter would start. Caro watched as Sophie pulled the band out of her ponytail then swept her hair, quick and rough, to the back of her head, before she twisted the band around her hair again. Ten seconds, if that. Compared to the twenty minutes she'd taken to get the ponytail right before they left home.

Next year, Caro thought, I'll come to netball every week.

Next year, Graeme will be here.

'If they do what I say, they'll be okay,' Heidi said, when she came back to the women and their chairs, but then United gave away the first three goals. Heidi sat back in her seat and scratched at the top of her head with both of her hands. Sophie pulled at her ponytail.

'It's all right, United,' Caro called. 'This one's yours.'

Oh. Yelling out like that, it even stretched your lips.

United got the next four, and then the goals went one for one.

Caro needed a cigarette. Really needed it.

Magpies goal. Magpies goal. United. United.

Magpies. A miss by United. Magpies end, no goal, United end, no goal.

Caro could smell someone's cigarette. A quick look around, but she couldn't see who it was.

United missed another goal.

Caro stood up from her seat, then muttered, 'Excuse me, excuse me, excuse me, sorry,' as she walked, back and shoulders hunched until she got to the edge of the crowd.

Another goal against United. Half the crowd roared, half groaned.

By the time I get back, Caro promised herself, it will all be over.

Caro took purposeful strides to the toilet block, then, with a quick look around, she sidestepped the door and walked around the building until she could stand, back against the wall, light a cigarette and take a long, deep drag.

More cheers and shouts from the other side of the toilet block. Another drag.

'Oh, hello.'

Caro jumped, then looked towards the voice. It was Heidi's friend. The one who'd just had the baby. What was her name? Brooke? Rebecca? She was dressed, like Heidi, in a navy blue box-pleat skirt, red polo shirt and socks.

'Great minds,' the girl – young woman – said, then lit her own cigarette. Menthol.

Caro took another drag.

'Think alike I mean.'

She was looking at Caro and Caro felt she had to smile. Another cheer, louder this time.

'I hope they win, don't you?'

Is even a quick, quiet smoke behind the toilet block too much to ask?

'Especially if this is gonna be Heids' last game here. I hope those kids she's coaching win, and I hope we win the A grade this afternoon. And I hope she gets the best and fairest at the presentation next week.' She took a drag on her cigarette. 'Don't you?'

'Oh, yes,' Caro said.

'I don't want anyone to let her down. Not this time.'

The girl took two quick drags on her cigarette then flicked quickly at its end, four, five, six times, then took another drag.

From time to time the girl looked towards the corner of the building. 'If she knows I've been smoking, she'll be mad.' She was flicking at her cigarette again. 'She give you a hard time about it? About your smoking?'

'Do you mean Heidi?' Caro asked, and when the girl nodded, Caro shook her head. 'No.'

The girl kicked at the ground a few times before she spoke again.

'You don't remember me, do you?'

'Oh, yes. Heidi introduced us. Before you had your baby.' She'd bumped into them in Foodland. Or Coles. Just a few days after she'd arrived. Not long after she'd met Heidi. This is my best friend, Heidi had said. But the name was still nowhere to be found. Bianca? Briony?

'We met before that. Ages ago. At Joel's twenty-first. Joel went as the chicken and I was the egg.'

'Oh. Renee.' She managed to leave the question mark off, but was that it? Were they both the same Renee? 'Yes, I remember. Just didn't recognise you without your shell and your yolk.' She remembered the costume. A kind of white vinyl that sagged so that the girl – someone, was it Libby, had introduced them – looked less like an egg and more like a balloon that was losing its helium.

'I was sorry about Sean. I've been wanting to tell you that. Ever since you came. I couldn't say when Heidi was there. But I wanted to let you know, I was really sad that he died.'

Libby must have told her about all this. She must have told her they were the same Renee. Caro remembered a bit more about it now. An engagement made then broken and luckily the invitations hadn't been printed although the caterer's deposit had been paid. But had Libby told her this? Surely. Surely she had.

'He was such a lovely man.'

'Yes,' Caro said, only because it would have been rude to let the silence sit any longer.

'So different to Joel, wasn't he?'

Caro nodded.

'Oh. That sounds terrible. I don't mean that Joel wasn't . . . isn't . . . I just mean . . . just, you know, Sean was so much more "what you see is what you get" than Joel. Do you know what I mean?'

What you see is what you get. Caro would add it to the list. It could come just after 'salt of the earth' and just before 'heart of gold'.

'I wanted to go to his funeral, but then when Heids decided not to go, it seemed wrong for me to go. Do you know what I mean?'

Another call from the crowd. Not a cheer or a shout. An umpire's decision gone wrong perhaps.

'Funny to think we could've been sister-in-laws. Don't you think?'

Caro gave a non-committal smile. Three drags left. She could make it two. She could put it out now if she wanted to. Tell the girl she had to go. She didn't want to miss the end of the game.

'If we were . . .' The girl took a quick drag. 'If we were

sister-in-laws, would you be telling me what to do? Would you be telling me to leave?'

More shouts and cheers.

'I haven't . . .' Hasn't anyone around here heard about doctor-patient confidentiality? 'Doctors don't tell people what to do. Doctors give advice and information and offer options and support people in their decisions. Doctors don't tell people what to do.'

They each put their cigarettes to their lips, but Caro's drag was deeper.

'There's not that many times that people haven't been telling Heidi what to do,' the girl – Renee – said, and held Caro's eye until Caro dropped her final drag on the ground, twisting her foot hard over the butt.

'I'd better get back to the game,' she said. 'Good luck this afternoon.'

And then, as Caro rounded the corner, she heard the final siren and saw across the courts, the United mothers jumping up, hugging each other.

Forty-nine netball courts surrounded by cyclone wire and around them, a harness racing track that charged two dollars admission, a train line that never got used, a panel beating shop that was always full. A clear blue sky, the sun on the back of her neck, bottle brushes already fully bloomed.

Caro turned, faced Renee again.

'I told her she could always come back. I told her if it doesn't work out and she wants to come back, it doesn't mean she's failed.'

CHAPTER THIRTY-TWO

The house could do with a lick of paint, Heidi thought as she looked at it from the car. Dad would have to get busy.

'Wave to Pop,' she said to Zac, and stopped the car for a moment as she backed the car onto the road. Dad looked smaller than ever before. He lifted his arms above his head, pumped them up and down like wings. Then he put his thumbs in his ears, wiggled his fingers up and down, poked his tongue in and out. Zac laughed.

One last wave. It was too early to push the horn, so she said it instead as she drove away. 'Beep beep beepity-beep, goodbye street.'

She felt a fluttering. It was the baby now for sure.

She thought of driving past Joel's place. If she went to him now, told him she could feel the baby moving, would he have a proper answer, or would he still be making excuses. I need to stay for Mum's birthday. I promised Jammo I'd help him scrape the barnacles off his boat. The car needs a service before I take it anywhere. Shep's buck's night is already planned.

He had made promises.

They said they'll hold the job for me until the end of the month. I've rung them and they've said it's okay. I'll be two weeks at the most. He had kissed her cheek, then lightly brushed against her lips and Heidi had nodded like she believed, but still she wasn't sure.

And all of that was before he found out she'd been to Robbo's funeral.

She didn't regret going. But would it be different if she'd been the one to tell Joel? Or if she hadn't taken the seat that Vicki had saved for her, down the front, second pew back so Zac could sit with Helen's kids?

Would it be different if she hadn't kissed Brad?

A simple kiss, nothing more than a brushing of his cheek, no more or less than anyone else had done. But he had held her closer then than she had ever been held before. The memory of him holding her lingered in her thoughts and got tangled in her words. Every extra thing she said to Joel just made things worse.

Back and forth her and Joel had gone. Robbo was his grandfather. I needed you at Sean's. I would have gone, but Libby made it clear, Zac wasn't welcome there.

She turned left, then left again and smiled at herself for chucking a mainie first thing in the morning. She wound down the window and drove slowly to get a better look at all she was leaving. It didn't matter how slow she was at this time of the day. There was no one around to care.

Heidi had never properly noticed the iron lace of the main street balconies before. Some of the balconies were painted black, but most were painted white. Black or white the iron lace was beautiful. Graceful. That was the word.

'See the animals, Zac?' she said. She had never pointed out the three heads carved in stone across the top of the butcher's shop. A pig, a cow and a sheep. Mum used to point at them every week, but Heidi had stopped noticing them a long time ago, more or less forgotten they were there. She pointed, then turned quickly to look at him, but he was looking the other way. He'd probably noticed them some-time anyway. Kids did. Kids noticed everything.

The baby moved again. Heidi straightened her back and pushed into her seat. It would not be a comfortable drive. Two hours would seem like five. She should have brought a cushion to slip in at the base of her back.

It would only take a minute, she thought, to go back home and grab one. Dad wouldn't mind if she took the red cushion from the couch.

Had Mum remembered everything? The day she left. Were there any last-minute things? Is that why Mum had last been seen only an hour before Heidi would have got home? Because she'd forgotten the fingernails, the school photo-graphs, the sewing machine, and she'd had to turn around? But she'd taken so few things. Or maybe she'd never planned to leave, just been hit with the whim one afternoon, gathered a few things up and driven off?

Heidi took a hand off the steering wheel and rubbed at her eyes.

One last drive along the wharf. She turned left and stopped at the railway line, although it only said 'Give Way'. She looked left, then right, then left again. As if she wouldn't hear the train. As if she had to double-check. As if there could be a train running along the wharf.

'Oh, there's no ships in,' she said. Zac didn't reply.

She got a hint of the mix of the sulphur and the sea in the air. She drove past the slag heaps and past the cranes and past the peeps of the smelters you could still get through the fence. The furnace flames, steel carts on wheels, a man in a white hard hat.

At the end of the wharf Heidi stopped the car, got out, leaned against the bonnet. Have the silos always been that white? Who painted them? And how? It would be a big job and everyone would be talking about it. There'd be pictures in the paper. So why didn't she know?

The baby fluttered. She rubbed her stomach, took the deepest breath she could. 'It's all right, little one,' she said. 'You just go to sleep.'

She rubbed at her stomach again.

You'll be needing a name soon, won't you?

She looked to the other end of the wharf where the fishing boats were moored. The big boats were out, and most of the small ones too. It would be beautiful out in a boat today. Not too windy and not too hot. Not bad for this time of year.

She thought of the days when Dad still had the boat and she went out with him to tan her legs and help pull the crab nets in. Back home, they'd light a fire in the backyard and if Dad was using the big black pot, they'd watch the crabs go from blue to red. Beautiful, she'd thought, until she understood what the colour change meant.

She might never do that again. Watch the crabs change colour.

She looked out towards the sea where the 'Missions to Seamen' sign was nailed into its board, its paint faded and chipped.

Lord, my ship is so small and your sea is so big. We are as near to heaven by sea as by land!

In all the times she had read that sign, this was the first time she understood.

You can be spooked by the things that you love.

'Mum?' It was Zac's voice from the car. 'When are we going?'

She got back into the car, left the wharf, turned back into the street. Were there really so many palm trees down the centre of the road? She counted them as she drove. One, two, three, four . . . twenty-two from the wharf to here, plus all the others before that. Probably fifty in all.

'Just one last look at the beach,' she said. 'Then we'll get going.'

The small jetty they had jumped from when they were kids. The stone wall where they sat on Friday nights because there was nowhere else to go when you were too young for the pub. Brad on one side, Renee on the other. Passing cigarettes and wine coolers back and forth. Wine coolers and some-times Malibu.

Across the creek, the mangrove swamps where her canoe got stuck in that week of outdoor ed.

You'll have to get out, Mr Edwards had said. And getting

out was worse than being stuck. The grey mud frightened her, but she wouldn't let herself cry because Mr Edwards would let everyone know.

She turned the car again, drove back to the main road, turned left. She checked the tally sign at the front of the petrol storage tanks just like she always did. Days without incident on this site: 408. It had got to 622 once, but she didn't know how much further it got, because the next time she looked it was back to 27 and like Dad said after all that time, you couldn't be sure that there had only been one accident or whether there'd been two or three in the space of a week like there sometimes was.

She wondered now, like she had wondered then, What had the accident been?

There was the sign – 'Thank you for visiting. Come back and see us soon' – and Renee's car parked next to it. Heidi had always liked Renee's numberplate. EFG765. She had told Renee about the pattern once, how the letters went up while the numbers went down, but she should have known that patterns are something you can't explain.

Renee was standing next to the driver's side, waving Heidi down.

'I'll have to stop,' Heidi said to Zac. 'But I'm not getting out.'

She pulled over, put the car in neutral and wound the window down without turning the engine off.

Renee walked to the car, bent down, looked through Heidi's window. 'You're not taking much,' she said. Her hair was pulled back in a ponytail, and she wasn't wearing any make-up, but she looked like she'd had a good night's sleep.

'The boot's full,' Heidi said.

She did not have to explain her last-minute fear that she would pack the poison and bring it with them in the car so that in the end, she had unpacked nearly everything she had already packed, and washed the things she couldn't leave behind before she carried them in sealed bags and covered boxes out to the car. Some photos in frames, a few of her books, enough clothes for Zac, and even those she thought she would throw out when she got a chance to buy some more. 'And the house is furnished,' she said. 'It's got beds and chairs and everything.'

'I can't believe you're going,' Renee said.

'Neither can I.'

'And Joel still reckons he'll be there in two weeks?'

Heidi nodded, then shrugged.

Renee looked at Zac, then back to Heidi again.

To break the look between them, Heidi said, 'You'll visit me, won't you? When the baby's born maybe?'

'Course,' Renee said. 'And you'll ring me when you get there? Let me know you got there safe?'

Heidi nodded.

She accidentally revved the engine.

'You haven't forgotten my dream, have you?' Renee asked. 'The one I told you about when you first got back? With the baby and you.'

'No,' Heidi said, although until that moment she had forgotten. Actually, no, that wasn't right. She might have forgotten the dream, but she hadn't forgotten its meaning.

Renee was looking back towards the town. 'Leaving wouldn't work for me,' she said. 'I wouldn't belong anywhere else.' Then she leaned back into the car, kissed Heidi on the cheek. 'See you later.'

'See you,' Heidi said.

She waited for Renee to step out of the way, then edged the car back on the road and waved goodbye. Renee blew her another kiss.

Heidi pressed the accelerator down.

'Now we're on our way,' she said to Zac.

The sky was clear and blue. Across the saltbush flats, the Flinders Ranges stretched on either side and if she didn't look in the rear-vision mirror, she wouldn't see the stack as she drove away.